MW00479876

ABE

SAVAGE KINGS MC NOVEL

LANE HART

D.B. WEST

ABE

A SAVAGE KINGS MC NOVEL

NEW YORK TIMES BESTSELLING AUTHOR
LANE HART
D.B. WEST

COPYRIGHT

This book is a work of fiction. The characters, incidents, and dialogue were created from the authors' imagination and are not to be construed as real. Any resemblance to actual people or events is coincidental.

The authors acknowledge the copyrighted and trademarked status of various products within this work of fiction.

© 2018 Editor's Choice Publishing

All Rights Reserved.

Only Amazon has permission from the publisher to sell and distribute this title. This book or any portion thereof may not be reproduced or used in any manner whatsoever without the express written permission of the publisher except for the use of brief quotations in a book review.

Editor's Choice Publishing

P.O. Box 10024

Greensboro, NC 27404

Edited by Angela Snyder
Cover by Marianne Nowicki of PremadeEbookCoverShop.com

WARNING: THIS BOOK IS NOT SUITABLE FOR ANYONE UNDER 18. PLEASE NOTE THAT IT CONTAINS SCENES THAT MAY BE A TRIGGER FOR INDIVIDUALS WHO HAVE BEEN IN SIMILAR SITUATIONS.

CHAPTER ONE

Mercy Daniels

THE REAL WORLD SUCKS.

As soon as I step through the doors of the pier restaurant, I feel dozens of eyes on me and have to fight the urge to turn around and run. The lunch crowd is looking at me with sympathy; because even a year later, I'm still just Mercy, the aptly named, pathetic woman who had her heart snapped in half on a reality television show.

Okay, maybe I'm just imagining the pitiful stares, and pathetic is simply how I still see myself every time I look in the mirror. After traveling the world for an entire year with my overbearing, Bible-thumping mother to avoid standing still long enough for the paparazzi to take a photo, I thought I would be over the pain and humiliation.

Guess not.

"Mercy!"

The sound of my former college roommate's comforting voice grounds me, pulling me out of my self-conscious thoughts. I've missed Sasha and could really use a friend right now. Lifting my big sunglasses that I use as a shield to keep my emotions from pouring out of my eyes, I finally spot my tall, blonde friend when she stands up and waves. Not only does she grab my attention, but everyone else in the restaurant as well. Sasha is a beautiful woman who simply radiates warmth, so all eyes are definitely on us now.

I hurry over to the table she's claimed for us and give her a hug.

"Hey, girl!" Sasha says as we embrace. "It's been too long, as in an entire calendar year! I've missed you!"

"I know, and I'm sorry. I missed you too," I tell her as I take a seat across from her. Removing my sunglasses from the top of my head, I slip them into my purse and then hang it on the back of my chair.

"I've been worried about you," she says softly.

"Oh, I'm fine," I reply with a wave of my hand. "And I didn't mean to drop off the map from everyone, but it seemed like the only way to escape the drama was to keep moving," I explain. "After the first few weeks, I think I was scared to call and have someone bring *him* up and make my heart break all over again when I was trying so hard to get over him."

"No, I totally understand," Sasha assures me, reaching across the table to give my hand a squeeze. "And I won't ask you about *He-Who-Shall-Not-Be-Named*. But I'm here if you want to talk about it."

"Thanks, I appreciate that," I tell her with a small smile.

"You look great, by the way," she says.

"Thanks, you too! Running has become my new best friend," I admit. "The only time I could really get away from my mother while we traveled."

"I noticed you've been making some headlines too," Sasha responds. "Is it true? Are you going to be the new leading lady on *Queen of Hearts* this season?"

"I am," I answer with a nod.

"Congrats?" Sasha asks with a wince as if she's not sure if it's a good thing or not.

"Yeah, I mean it's a great opportunity to try and meet Mr. Right and move on from Mr. Wrong," I say, trying to convince myself that's true as I open the restaurant's plastic menu and lower my eyes to study it.

"Are you sure you're ready to date again?" Sasha asks, her voice lowered in concern.

"Yes, of course," I tell her, looking over the menu with a smile. "It's been over a year. Besides, what woman wouldn't want to be the object of twenty incredibly hot men's attention?"

"One who is still in love with someone else who cheated on her and ran his mouth about her to the world," she whispers to herself as she pretends to look at her own menu.

Closing mine, since I always have the grilled chicken salad, I rest my forearms on top of it to reply to her comment. "It was a show. Did I think Blake was going to pick me at the finale? Absolutely. But he didn't. And while my ego took a huge hit after the show aired, seeing him on camera with all those other women and talking about how bad I am in bed, it has now healed. My heart too."

"If you say so," Sasha replies with a shrug of her shoulders, pretending she's buying my explanation and letting it go. After all, that's what best friends are for.

"So, tell me what you've been up to," I say to effectively change the topic.

"Well," Sasha starts, then tosses her menu down so that she can hold out her left hand to show off her ring. "I'm engaged!"

"Holy shit," I mutter when I grasp her hand to bring it closer while examining the massive diamond. "That's a beautiful ring. Who is the lucky groom-to-be?" I ask, excited that my friend has at least found a keeper. In my heart, I thought that Blake was going to put a ring on my finger when instead he said I wasn't the one for him.

"You remember me telling you about Chase Fury, my high school sweetheart?" Sasha asks.

"Of course," I remark. How could I forget the name of the jerk she used to cry over at various times through our four years of college after he abandoned her when he wrecked his bike?

"Well, it turns out that he *was* there for me after our accident, for days, in fact; and my parents told him that I didn't want to see him and that I blamed him for everything," she says. "They intentionally split us up! And because I was too stubborn to talk to him, we didn't find all that out until a few weeks ago."

"Wow," I reply in surprise. "So, how did you get back together?"

"It's a long story, but I reported on an accident where he was the man police were looking for," she says. A waiter appears beside our table to get our orders before I can ask a follow up.

As soon as we're alone again, I say, "Go back. The man's *a criminal?*"

"Ah, sort of," Sasha replies with a wrinkle of her nose. "Like I said, it's a long story, but the best part is that we're back together. And to be completely honest with you, you should know that he's the acting president of the Savage Kings MC right now. So, associating with me could not only be bad PR for you but also...dangerous."

"Ha!" I laugh since there's no way I'm staying away from my best friend I haven't seen in a year because her bad boy biker fiancé could be trouble. "Bring it on!" I tell her. "It would actually be great to have the paparazzi report something about me that doesn't have to do with...well, you know."

Everyone always thinks that those reality shows are staged and scripted, but the truth is, I fell hard for Blake, the bachelor from last season's show *King of Hearts*. Sure, I knew that I would be competing with nineteen other women when I signed a contract. As a struggling model-slash-small time actress, I needed the money and thought it would be great for publicity. And I was right. Now I'm known as the woman who told a man she loved him after he professed his love. A few days later, I then proceeded to push him into a pool when he picked another woman at the final rose ceremony. That's right, every second of my jealous fit is out there for the world to see. And although the cameras left before we got naked, everyone also knows that Blake and I had been sleeping together for three weeks prior to him choosing Felicia, a woman he barely spent any time with other than in bed. At the recent reunion show, tempers flared and insults ensued, including an accusation that I was colder than an Alaskan trout in the sack. Blake declared that he realized before the ceremony that I was faking everything I said and did with him to try and keep myself on the show for my failing career.

Asshole.

The only thing fake between us were my orgasms that he failed to ever give me because he was a selfish prick. Which I could have overlooked if he had loved me.

Let's just say that on top of the pile of trust issues my absentee father created, Blake caused me to develop a few new ones. There's a reason I haven't been on a date with anyone in over a year, and that reason's name is Blake fucking Burton. Because of him, I can't stop thinking what if he's right and I *am* solely responsible for having never experienced good sex?

"Seriously, Mercy. There have been some attacks on the club, and the guys are on the rampage after Chase's sister-in-law was killed by one of their enemies," Sasha tells me, pulling me back into our conversation. "If you want to steer clear of me, I'll understand."

"That's awful," I reply. "And while I hate that happened, I don't think our friendship will be hazardous to my health."

"I hope not," Sasha says. "I would feel terrible if something happened to you because of my association with Chase and the MC, but I'm glad that you think I'm worth it."

"Definitely," I agree, right before several bright flashes of light go off right outside the window next to our table.

I don't even have to look out on the deck to know what's going on, but Sasha does.

"Jesus!" she mutters when her jaw falls open and she looks back at me.

"So, there are a few hazards of being friends with me right now too," I warn her. "Like the fact that you're probably going to end up in the tabloids as my lesbian lover or something equally absurd."

Sasha gives a big burst of laughter at that. "I can see it now, once they do a little digging and find out we were roommates in college.

The headlines will probably be that we've been secret lesbian lovers for years and today we finally outed ourselves." When she starts giggling again, I can't help but join in.

"Thanks for having a sense of humor about this," I tell her. "They have been all up in my ass worse than an epic wedgie since I got back into town a few days ago. I hope it doesn't cause you any problems with the news station."

"Oh, please," she says with a wave of her hand. "I figured they would fire me as soon as I went public with Chase, but they've actually been kissing my ass instead, like they're scared I'll sic the MC on them if they try to let me go."

"That's great," I tell her.

"It is. I have my pick of stories, more vacation time. It's crazy, but I'm glad I didn't have to give up my career to be with Chase."

"Yeah, it's awesome you get to have both," I agree with a smile.

"Are you gonna be in town for a while? If you are, I really want you to meet him," Sasha says.

"Absolutely," I reply. "We start filming later this week in Wilmington. It'll take weeks to get a season worth of bad dates and all filmed, so I'll be around."

"Bad dates?" Sasha repeats with a bark of laughter. "Try not to sound so hopeful!"

"You know what I mean," I say with a roll of my green eyes. "The guys may all be hot, but some will be jackasses. I just have to focus on weeding those men out, which will take time. And in the meantime, I'm going to try to avoid the paparazzi as much as I can."

"How exactly do you plan to get out of here with that growing horde outside?" she asks, tipping the side of her head toward the window. I don't turn to acknowledge the cameras. I'm trying my best to avoid letting them get any straight-on shots of my face looking like a deer in headlights.

Glancing around the restaurant that's also filled with gawkers now, I grin and say, "Maybe someone can find me a broom to beat them back with."

"I have a better idea," Sasha says with her own mischievous grin. I can't even guess what she might be cooking up. The girl is as sweet as honey, but can occasionally be trouble with a capital T. "If you don't mind the MC association, I could call in a few bikers to provide you with some backup."

"Bikers?" I repeat before my eyes narrow at her. "Wait. You're not trying to set me up, are you? I'm getting ready to start a dating show!"

"Of course I'm not setting you up. None of Chase's friends even come close to being your type," she replies.

"Right," I agree, since I could never imagine myself dating a biker or my mother ever approving of one.

CHAPTER TWO

Abram Cross

THIS DUDE HAS LOST HIS FUCKING MIND.

That's my first thought when Chase and I show up at Torin's house to check on him. And while I can't imagine what it would be like to have to walk a mile in his boots, I have zero fucking doubts that he's experiencing more pain than any human being ever should endure in a lifetime.

A few weeks ago, motherfucking Hector Cruz, Cartel drug king-pin, had someone take out Torin's pregnant old lady in a drive-by. The entire club is still reeling from the attack on our president. Or our *former* president, I guess I should say, since he removed his flash from his cut and stepped down.

Now, though, he's set up camp right next to his beach front mansion...in a fox hole. No shit, it's like he's reenacting a war movie. The man hasn't seen a bar of soap in several days, possibly longer, not to mention a razor or a comb for his dirty-blond hair that's a mess, falling below his ears and giving new meaning to *dirty*.

It's just one more reason why I never plan to settle down with a woman. Not that any females would ever want to hitch themselves to me – a convicted felon and outlaw biker – other than the low-class club sluts. They're bottom feeders looking to move up in the world even if it means getting on their knees for me every night. And it's no secret that the MC is making bank. The amount of money in my account is a dream come true compared to how I grew up saving pennies or stealing to pay for one meal a day for my mom, my brother and myself.

"Come on, Torin," Chase starts, trying to rationalize with his older brother from where he and I are physically looking down into the depths of his despair. Actually, the more I think about it, instead of a fox hole, it's like the man has gone and dug his own grave to prepare for his imminent death, ready to meet back up with his old lady in the afterlife. "Why don't you go inside and get a shower? Or come back to the clubhouse with us?"

"No," Torin mutters from his seated position, back to the sandy wall. "I'm fine here."

"You're not fucking fine!" Chase yells before he places his hands on his hips to take a deep breath, trying to calm down. As his MC brother, I understand his frustration. Hell, I even understand the pressure Chase has on his shoulders, wanting to literally pull Torin out of the hole he's dug himself into. My brother Gabriel is three years younger than me; and when I lost him to the foster system those few years after our mom died, I felt like a failure. When I was finally able to track him down again, I thought it would be smart to steal a classic Jaguar to sell to pay for his college tuition. Then I got busted and tossed in prison, leaving Gabe once again to fend for himself. I'm a shitty brother. And based on the distance between us despite our close proximity, I don't think he's ever forgiven me for letting him down.

"There has to be something more that you could be doing than wasting away out here in the heat," Chase says calmly, trying to reason with his brother. "What do you need?"

"Have you found out where Hector or his slutty ass daughter

are?" Torin murmurs. "Yeah, I didn't think so," he answers his own question before Chase can respond.

"We're trying," Chase assures him. "Reece is digging in and monitoring everything possible that he can on the internet. We'll find them."

Straight up, that murdering asshole Cruz must be hiding in a hole like Torin's. There hasn't been a single blip about him out in the world since he closed up shop in Wilmington and disappeared after attacking our clubhouse and killing two good men from our Charlotte charter.

"We can try to round up some Aces again to question them," Chase offers to Torin, trying to throw the devastated man a bone.

"I want to burn the entire Ace of Spades MC to the fucking ground," Torin declares while he pulls out his big ass army knife from his cargo pocket to start cutting an apple.

Chase and I exchange a look, then I give a shrug in response to his silent question as if to say, why the hell not.

"Okay, let's do it," Chase tells him. "Let's burn that fucking Aces' bar right outside of Wilmington down. We'll go tonight."

"Fuck yeah," I exclaim, trying to be the messed-up arson cheerleader my boy needs.

"Fine," Torin eventually agrees with a sigh.

"Great. Get a shower and you can come too," Chase declares. When Torin opens his mouth to protest, Chase cuts him off. "I can fucking smell you from here, man. If you don't shower, you're not coming with us."

A huff of annoyance is Torin's response, but Chase seems to take it as acceptance.

"Be at the clubhouse at eleven tonight," Chase orders Torin before he walks away. I give my former president a nod, before I turn and follow. The whole exchange was too damn bizarre for me. Over the past six years since I became a prospect, Torin's been the one in charge giving people directives. Seeing him this way twists my guts up in knots.

"Are you gonna tell him about the possible rat in our midst?" I ask Chase softly as we head for our bikes.

"Not yet," Chase answers on a sigh. "He'll lose it if we tell him one of our own betrayed him. First we need to find proof before *he* goes apeshit and starts pointing fingers."

"Yeah," I agree, unable to figure out how the hell to determine which of our brothers is untrustworthy.

Growing up poor made me hard. Prison made me even harder. Chase was the only person in there with me who I knew wouldn't stab me with a shiv while I was sleeping. I've always had a hard time trusting people; but even so, I've gone through the list of our MC brothers over and over again and can't pick out a single one who *wouldn't* die for me. Maybe Chase is wrong, and Hector just got lucky when he hit us both times. But that doesn't really make sense either ...

Just as Chase and I are next to our bikes, fastening our helmets, his cell phone starts ringing.

I'm going to go out on a limb here and throw out a guess that it's his old lady. The two of them can't go thirty minutes without professing their love. Chase can act like he's all happy and shit, but I see the worry on his face every time he's in the same room with Sasha. He's terrified of losing her like Torin lost Kennedy. Hell, Chase almost did ten years ago when a drunk driver wrecked his bike while Sasha was on the back. And honestly, I want my boy to be happy, but I just don't see how battling all that added fear is worth the trouble.

"Hey, sweetheart," Chase says into the phone with a goofy grin on his face, that I also predict is exactly the one Sasha shares wherever the hell she is right now. When his face hardens and his brow dips in concern, I get the feeling there's trouble in paradise.

"Where are you?" he snaps, and then says, "We're on our way," before ending the call.

"What's up?" I ask as Chase slips the phone back in the inside zipper on his cut and climbs on his bike.

"Sasha and her friend were having lunch and started getting hassled by some dicks with cameras," he explains. "We're gonna go break up the party."

"Sounds fun," I tell him before I throw a leg over my shiny, new Harley Street Glide, ready to ride.

I owe Chase big time for being so cool with me in prison and then giving me and Gabriel a home after I got out. The Savage Kings MC is the first real family the two of us have ever had. Sure, Gabriel spent a few years in several foster homes; and although he doesn't talk about them, I don't think it was a very good experience for him. Hell, I have no idea how Gabe was even surviving when a private investigator was finally able to track him down in the streets of Charlotte.

Thankfully, while I was locked up, my brother met an older man named Tom Wright, who had his own tattoo shop, and the dude let Gabe apprentice with him. That's how my brother was able to open up his shop in Emerald Isle when we both moved here to join the MC six years ago. I hate I couldn't round up the money he needed to go to college and get his art degree or whatever, but I'm so fucking proud of him. Maybe I'm biased, but my brother is hands down the sickest fucking artist in the world. Not just with tattoos; he can draw damn near anything. He did the sleeve of black and white roses on my arm and the MC bearded skull patch on my back. He inks almost all of the guys in the MC. People even travel from out of state to get a Gabriel Cross tat.

My brother was born with an incredible talent, and I was born... big. That's it. That's the extent of my attributes. I'm a stubborn, hard-headed giant, but I can follow orders and wouldn't hesitate to put a bullet in someone to protect one of my MC brothers. Especially Chase. He's a good guy, and I'm glad that the angry bastard finally got his girl. The man practically floats on air now, and I don't think any dude smiles as much as he does, even if that fear never leaves his eyes.

He's not smiling when we back in our bikes into parking spots at the Sea Breeze pier restaurant and turn off the engines. And he's not smiling as he pushes his way through the crowd of dickheads staring into one of the windows like they're on a field trip at the damn zoo.

"What's the matter with these people?" I grumble to Chase, who reaches the door to go inside a step before me.

"No fucking idea, but somehow Sasha has gotten herself involved," he replies over his shoulder, which I translate to mean he's gonna kick some ass if they don't back the fuck up.

I'm still snickering to myself about how much fun it'll be to see my boy throw down with the nerds with cameras when I glance around the dining room and see *her* turn around, stunning me so severely with her intense emerald eyes and red, flowing hair that I nearly stumble backwards.

Correction, it should be HER. The woman deserves to have the entire word capitalized because she's that fucking important. I don't know who the fuck SHE is, but everyone better get the fuck out of my way so I can find out.

And today must be my lucky day, or my boy must be appeasing my love of gingers, because Chase stops at HER table.

Jesus. The closer I get, the more stunning she is — all smooth, porcelain skin that glows and makes those big, green eyes and fiery hair stand out even more.

Conversations take place around me, but I can't hear them. Chase says something. But nope, it doesn't register. I don't have a clue what's being said, or what's going on around us. I have perfect tunnel vision. I start to think my gawking is making HER uncomfortable because SHE keeps tilting her head back to look at me, and then quickly glancing away.

When Chase's arm shoots into my field of vision and shakes her hand, I have to choke back my growl of jealousy because he's being allowed to touch HER when I haven't. Hell, someone as classy and perfect wouldn't let my grungy hands ever come close to her. Still, a man can fantasize and jerk off to women way out of his league.

As soon as the goddess opens her mouth, I'm all ears.

"Nice to meet you. I'm Mercy."

"*Mercy?*" I repeat aloud with a chuckle. "As in, *Lord, please have Mercy on me?*"

The beauty throws her head back and laughs like I've said the funniest fucking shit she's ever heard. The sound is brief but lovely, like tinkling wind chimes on a calm day.

"Yes, just like that," she answers. She hesitates a moment before she holds out her dainty hand in my direction, finally giving me permission to touch her. Since I can't possibly shake it with my big mitt without breaking it, I gently slip my palm underneath and lower my lips to brush them over her delicate knuckles. When I lick my lips and taste the mango of her lotion or body wash, I nearly groan.

"Abe," Chase mutters from beside me in a tone that says I need to get a fucking grip.

And hell, I know that I do. In all my life, I've never kissed a woman's knuckles, not just because it looks like a cheesy fucking come-on, but because in the Savage Kings MC culture, it means I'm giving her a higher status than myself, a King. Only old ladies deserve that much respect, not a woman I just met.

"So, your name is Abe?" Mercy asks me, making my eyes nearly roll back in my head from just the sound of my name coming from her lips. I also realize I'm still touching her. "It's nice to meet you," she adds before withdrawing her hand from mine. The woman probably can't wait to go wash off my germs. "Thanks for rescuing us from the rabid paps outside," she says with a nod of her red head toward the window. I look up and realize those fuckers are still gathered around and start to understand what a goldfish must feel like being in a bowl.

And at the word *rescue*, I can easily picture myself tossing Mercy over my shoulder and then carrying her out to my bike like a caveman. Would she then reward me for my heroism? My cock believes she would in my wettest dreams, so it gives a hardy nod of agreement.

"We have a basement entrance," an older man with white hair

says when he comes up to our table. "If Miss Daniels would like to sneak out that way. I do apologize for the intrusion on your meal."

How does this random man know her last name? Why are the assholes with cameras following her? I mean, it's entirely possible that she's started a riot based on her beauty alone, but I'm guessing there's another reason.

Obviously noticing my confused expression, Mercy says, "I was on a television show and have another one coming up. No biggie."

The fact that there's a mob waiting outside begs to differ with her modesty.

"Chase and I can go out the front and distract them while Abe takes Mercy through the basement," Sasha suggests from the other side of the table. Wait a second. When did Chase's old lady get here? Doesn't matter. I fucking love that woman for making the suggestion that I take Mercy.

"Sounds good," I tell her.

"Um, okay," Mercy agrees.

"Abe, why don't you take Mercy home on your bike, and Chase and I can follow in her car?" Sasha, the doll she is, adds, making me want to kiss her.

"That's not really necessary," Mercy says, trying to kill my dick's hopes and dreams.

"With the helmet on, they probably won't even know it's you," Sasha points out. "If you get in your car right now, someone could follow you home..."

"Ugh. That's true," Mercy agrees as she blows out a frustrated breath. "And I've been able to keep the address of my rental house a secret by leaving it in the landlord's name. It would suck to have them start smothering me there too."

"Hand me your car keys, girl, and let's get out of here," Sasha tells her as she holds out her hand, palm facing up in expectation.

A few moments pass where Mercy considers her options before she finally grabs up her purse and pulls out a set of keys. Handing them over to Sasha, she says, "I still drive a silver BMW, and I'll text you the address." She reaches for her phone next and starts typing.

"Got it," Sasha replies with a nod. "I'll drop it off, and then Chase can bring me back here on his bike to get my car. Easy."

As soon as I realize I'm nodding like a bobble head in agreement to this superb plan, I tense my neck to make it stop.

"You ever been on the back of a Harley before?" Sasha asks her friend as she puts down cash for the food on the table.

Mercy pushes the money away and adds her own before she answers. "No, I haven't. Should I be worried?" She looks to Sasha, then to Chase and finally me.

They both tell her no at the same time I say with a straight face, "Yes. It's incredibly dangerous. You should hold on to me like your life depends on it, because it very well may."

"Right," Mercy replies with a grin.

She then gets to her feet so that she's standing inches away from me, drowning me in her sweet, mango scent. She's taller than I expected, but still it's impossible to notice how much bigger I am than she is. I have at least eight inches on her and over a hundred pounds. Not looking the least bit intimidated, though, she cranes her neck up to say, "Let's go, big guy."

CHAPTER THREE

Mercy

SASHA AND CHASE'S DISTRACTION WORKS OUT PERFECTLY. THE giant in leather and I are able to sneak out through the basement entry. There were steps that go straight down between the tall slants holding the building up and to the sand dunes underneath. Not a single soul has noticed that we're on the way to the parking lot, assuming instead that I'm still inside.

And while I may not know this tough looking man that I'm leaving with, Sasha does; and I'm getting a good vibe from him. He's incredibly hot, the biggest, most muscular man I've ever met. Towering nearly a foot above my five-foot-eight height, his thick biceps straining against the fabric of his black tee under his leather cut look strong enough to lift a compact car. His chest is noticeably rock hard and massive before leading down to a lean waist. The jeans he's wearing are loose on his long legs but tight around his...package, accentuating that area nicely. Believe me, I got a nice long look since his crotch was eye-level while I was sitting at the table.

Abe is not my type at all since I prefer clean-cut guys. But I can admit that his thick, black beard that's long enough to tug on and the ink covering his entire right arm is bad boy sexy. Heck, every single inch of him is tough and ruggedly sexy. Although, it's very possible that my hormones are just so excited to be this close to an available male for the first time in over a year that they've put blinders over my eyes.

Wait a second. *Is* Abe available? Not that it even matters, because he's definitely not my type.

Still, when we get to Abe's bike, he places a helmet on my head and I take the opportunity to look for a ring that says he's taken, but don't find one.

I'm starting to think that, despite her assurances, Sasha *is* trying to play matchmaker because she thinks I need to get back in the saddle. And yes, I do agree, which is why I signed the contract for *Queen of Hearts*. But the guys on the show are open to a serious relationship while I'm certain that the big, bad biker in front of me is only looking for a pair of open legs, the more the merrier. And my crushed heart doesn't need to sustain any more damage.

Abe's large, slightly clumsy hands fight with the narrow chin strap to get it fastened on me.

"Since this is my first ride, will you take it slow for me?" I ask him as he works.

He gives a deep, rumbling chuckle before he answers. "This bike couldn't go slow if I wanted it to," he informs me. "But I'll keep you safe," he assures me before a long pause. One where his dark, nearly black eyes stare off into the distance as if he just had an important thought.

"Everything okay?" I ask.

"Just realized why Chase is such a pussy," he says with a shake of his head.

"Oh-kay," I mutter since I have no idea what that means, and I'm definitely not used to being around men with potty mouths. My mother would slap a man for using such a vile word in front of her.

"There," Abe tells me with a heavy sigh when the chin strap is secure. "Now hop on, Little Red, and we'll get out of here."

"Little Red?" I repeat with a grin.

"Yeah, as in Riding Hood," he clarifies as if it were obvious. "You're Little Red, and clearly I'm the Big Bad Wolf."

"Of course," I agree with a widening smile because he's too cute. Enormous and scary looking with his tats, black beard and leather, but still strangely enough, cute, especially when he opens his mouth. I'm not sure if I could ever predict what might come out.

I'll probably giggle for days whenever I think about his first words to me.

"Mercy?" he had asked in surprise when I introduced myself. "As in, Lord please have Mercy on me?"

All my life I've heard several versions of that particular joke, intending to be innuendo, but it was the way Abe said it, like the phrase was exactly what his dirty mind had been thinking before he learned my name.

After I figure out how to get one of my strappy heels over the seat and get situated on the bike, I tuck my navy-blue dress underneath my butt, glad that it's a longish style that comes down to my calves. Abe pulls out another half-helmet from the saddle bag. Taking my purse from my hand, he places it inside the compartment. As soon as he gets his helmet in place, he throws his long leg over the seat so fast and efficiently that it looks like he's done it a million times before. And it is hot. The bearded skull patch under the words "Savage Kings" just inches away from my face is a little terrifying, though.

"Now what?" I ask him.

Abe looks over his shoulder at me with a thick eyebrow raised before he says, "You're gonna have to come closer than that, Red."

"How close?" I ask.

"Keep coming and I'll tell you when," he replies.

I scoot toward him a few inches but apparently not enough.

"Keep coming," his gruff voice demands of me while his dark gaze simultaneously rakes upward from my crotch straddling the seat to my eyes. A shiver runs through my entire body at the sound of his voice or from the heat of his stare, maybe even the masculine smell of his leather and sweat mixing together now that I'm so close to him my thighs are nearly hugging his waist.

"Put your arms around my waist and lock them tight," Abe directs before he looks away.

The guy is so big that, in order for my hands to meet, I'll have to press the side of my face into his back.

"You sure?" I ask him. "I mean, couldn't I just put my hands on the side of the bike like this?" I demonstrate the move for him.

Abe barely spares me a glance before he answers. "Sure, you could," he agrees, making me exhale in relief. "If you want to fall off."

Crap.

Pushing past the awkwardness of hugging a man I just met from behind, I scoot forward again and put my arms around his waist to get it over with, clasping my right hand over my left.

Holy...wow! I wasn't expecting his stomach to feel so hard and warm underneath my left hand. As if he thinks he needs to impress me even more, I feel those washboard ab muscles suddenly tighten underneath my fingertips, causing a tightening in my own lower belly that I haven't felt in a very long time.

"You good?" Abe asks. "We need to go."

Glancing back over to the front of the restaurant, I see Chase and Sasha break free of the crowd.

"Yes," I say.

"Hold on tight," Abe reminds me before he cranks the motorcycle's loud engine. After he slips on a pair of sunglasses over his eyes, he pats my hands and then leans toward the handlebars.

"I need to give you my address!" I shout so he can hear me over the muffler.

"Yeah, you do," he says with a chuckle before the bike jerks forward, which means the momentum sends me backwards.

I don't have to be told twice about holding on tight to him. I clasp my hands snuggly together against his taut stomach just in time because we're zooming out of the restaurant lot and down the road at what would be a dangerous speed in even a completely enclosed vehicle.

When we go around the first curve, I'm certain that the last thing I'll remember about this world is kissing pavement before I leave it. I even consider unfriending Sasha on social media as soon as my feet touch the ground again.

But then the road straightens out. My shoulders finally begin to relax a little. The rest of my body eventually follows suit, and soon I'm even able to lift my head from Abe's back to watch the rows of trees in the swampy forest pass us by. The wind in my face takes my breath away at first, but it's also refreshing and invigorating. Like I'm flying free, a bird escaping the cage for the very first time.

Ironically enough, knowing you're so close to a horrendous death at any second makes you feel alive. Especially since you know you can only evade mortality for so long.

And who knew that motorcycles were like gigantic vibrators? The sensations it's putting off between my extremely neglected legs are a very welcome surprise to go along with their muscular owner. The scent of leather is also becoming a new aphrodisiac for me apparently.

By the time we take an exit off the highway to pull into a rest area minutes or hours later, my panties are damp, and I feel like I'm right on the verge of an incredibly embarrassing orgasm.

"You still back there, Red?" Abe teases me with a grin over his shoulder as he puts his boots on the pavement to back his bike into a parking spot while my arms remain locked around his waist.

"Yeah, I think so," I answer with a smile as I finally loosen my grip and let him go to sit back. "That was...fun."

"Glad to hear it," he replies before he climbs off and removes his sunglasses and helmet. "If you're ready to go home, you can give me the directions," he says, standing with his hip against the bike and his tree trunk size thigh pressed against my knee.

Am I ready to go home yet to my lonely little cottage? Not really.

Since I just started moving in, it doesn't feel quite like home to me just yet. For the last year, I've been traveling through Europe with my mom, something we both always wanted to do but never had enough money for until I was cast on *King of Hearts* last year. So at least one good thing came from looking like a fool for the whole world to see.

"I can give you my address, but you can take the long way there," I finally inform Abe.

"Sounds good," he agrees with what I'm pretty sure is a smirk peeking out from his thick facial hair.

Without thinking about it, I reach up to tug on the end of Abe's beard, making his dark eyes widen. "Doesn't this get hot in the summer?"

Clearing his throat, he strokes his hand over his beard and says, "Hell yeah, it does, but it also gets the ladies hot too."

"I bet," I say, even though I'm a little disappointed that he apparently has not one singular lady, but plural "ladies." Which is stupid since I don't even know the guy.

About that time, my eyes lower to actually read the black shirt that he's wearing underneath his open leather cut. There's a cartoon drawing of a bearded man wearing sunglasses. The words in white say, "Beard Rides", with ten cents written below it in the beard itself.

"Oh," I mutter when understanding finally dawns on me and I feel my face flush from thinking of this man's mouth between a woman's legs. Not just any woman, but I imagine it in between mine. Isolation and loneliness are solely responsible for stupid, crazy thoughts like that. When have I ever thought such a thing about a man I just met? Never, because it's very unladylike.

"Well, we better get back on the road. You wouldn't want to keep the ladies waiting," I tell Abe as I silently yell at my hormones to settle the hell down. In just a few days, I'll be surrounded by twenty amazing men who will all plot, scheme, and compete to get some one-on-one time with me. And will I be able to trust that any of them really want me for more than just a tumble in the sheets? Probably not, but it's possible I could find a decent guy.

"What ladies?" Abe asks several seconds later with his brow furrowed.

"The ladies that love the, um, beard," I tell him.

"There aren't any ladies waiting on me tonight," he replies.

"What about on other nights?" I ask as I look down and brush the invisible lint off my dress, even though it's none of my business. He's just a nice guy doing a friend a favor by dropping me off.

"I'm sure there are some...ladies back at our clubhouse, but I haven't been able to recall any of their names or faces since the moment I saw yours."

Jeez, he's laying it on thick for a guy I just met. And the worst part? It's totally working for him.

Again, my lack of physical contact in over a year is making me think things I really shouldn't. I'm not the type of woman who sleeps with a man I just met or has a one-night stand. I have more self-respect for myself, and I'm smart enough to know how those things end for women. It's never good. Even women who *think* they're just in some friends-with-benefits situations, deep down they're desperately hoping that the man will one day wake up and realize he's in love with her. That never, ever happens. The man just moves on to the next stupid, naïve woman. That's why I can't afford to do something so crazy just because I'm horny. Or lonely. Whatever. Besides, do I really want another man to experience an awful round of sex with someone as cold as me?

"Listen, Abe," I start. "I really appreciate you helping me out with the ride. And maybe I'm completely wrong about you, but I'm sort of on the rebound right now, so you shouldn't waste your time trying to get in my panties. It wouldn't be worth it..."

"So you've already thought about me in your panties?" the giant of a man asks with a smirk when he crosses his arms over his massive chest.

"No, I didn't say that," I reply with a scoff. And oh, my god.

We're now having an actual conversation about my panties and it's all my fault. "I said you shouldn't try to get in them, because I'm a lost cause."

"Are you wearing panties?" Abe asks me as his dark eyes lower to where my body is straddling his bike like he's trying to see through the material of my dress.

"What? Of course I am," I reply indignantly with a roll of my eyes, trying not to think about the dampness in them.

"Then the possibility of me getting in them, however slim it may be, is still there, right?" he points out.

Yes.

"Uh-uh. Nope," I disagree with an adamant shake of my head. I'm looking for love, not a chance to finally try and have wild, hot sex. There's a huge difference between the two. Letting the big man I just met have his way with me would not be conducive to building a relationship. However good it could possibly feel at the time, as soon as it's over and he walks away like every other man in my life, I'll feel ashamed of myself and regret my irrational decision. And it will most likely be terribly unfulfilling for both of us.

"There's no way to change your mind?" Abe asks. "I'd literally do *anything* to get in your panties just once. I promise to make it worth your while."

See! I knew it. He just admitted that all he wants from me is a one-night stand. And while I appreciate his candor, that's exactly what I'm trying like hell to avoid.

"Consider my panties a chastity belt of sorts. They're impossible to penetrate nowadays," I tell him.

Crap, why did I say penetrate? Now I'm thinking about sex with the giant when I'm supposed to be guiding the conversation away from sex. Having meaningless sex with a stranger would be wrong for so many reasons. At the moment, I can't think of any right off the top of my head, but I know they're out there in the world somewhere.

"Unless I find the key," Abe says.

"Huh?" I ask, having gotten caught up in the penetration issue.

"Those chastity belts from the Medieval Times had keys, didn't they?" he asks.

"I think you mean the Middle Ages," I reply, biting back my grin because he's thinking of the dinner theater place down south of us in Myrtle Beach. "And there was only one very special, hidden key, so it wasn't like just any old key would work."

"What if I know a damn good locksmith?" Abe asks with a cocky grin that makes me laugh out loud.

"You're funny, big guy, I'll give you that," I tell him with a shake of my head.

"So what's the deal with the rebound?" he asks, causing the smile to slip right off my face.

"It's nothing," I say. "And you're obviously not a fan of reality television or social media."

"Nope, I'm not," he replies.

"Well, then you're not missing much," I assure him. "I went on a dating show and thought the guy was going to propose to me at the finale. Instead, he picked another girl."

"Is he blind?" Abe asks. "The bastard's obviously fucking blind, right?"

"No," I answer, unable to bite back another grin. "He was not blind."

"Was he good in bed?"

"What? I'm not telling you that," I huff.

"So, he wasn't," Abe murmurs.

"I didn't say that."

"Because you're a sweet girl who wouldn't badmouth a man behind his back," he declares.

"Or I just don't go around bragging about my conquests," I argue.

"Did he give you beard rides?" Abe asks entirely straight faced as he tugs on his beard, making me laugh even harder because he looks so serious.

"Oh my, god. You're too much," I tell him. "Take me home."

"Answer the question and I will," he says when he plants one of his gigantic hands on the seat of the bike, his fingertips disappearing underneath the stretched fabric of my dress, not touching me but so close I can practically feel them.

Since I don't have much of a choice but to reply or walk, I decide to tell him the truth, even though I know I could lie to him. For some reason, I think he would know and not budge until he got the truth.

"No beard rides," I respond. Then, with a slight smile I say, "He was clean-shaven."

"Oh, come on!" Abe exclaims as he pushes off from the bike, then turns around in a circle and comes right back. His planted hand disappears a little further up the seat under my dress but still doesn't touch me. "Answer the question, woman."

"Why do you care?" I ask him curiously.

"Because any man who turns down the chance to lick your pretty, red pussy should be castrated," he grumbles.

My lips part on a gasp of surprise at his filthy words describing a very intimate place on my body. I like them, maybe even too much. No man has ever spoken to me in such a crass way.

"How...how do you know I'm a natural redhead?" I ask.

"Just taking an educated guess," Abe replies, letting his hand slip forward a little more. How do I know? Another gasp escapes my lips when his thumb grazes along the inside of my thigh and then stays there to keep rubbing up and down, up and down, stealing my breath with each small movement. "I'm all for taking a peek to confirm."

My mouth is so dry that I have to lick my lips before I can reply. I shouldn't encourage him, but for some reason I can't help myself. "Most of the time even a peek wouldn't do you any good because I usually get Brazilian waxes. But I may have missed a few appointments..."

"Good lord," Abe groans as his dark eyes squeeze shut as if he's trying to picture what I look like down below. His thumb on my thigh doesn't pause for even a second, though. It's singularly responsible for causing my entire lower body to start to tingle. In my head, my hormones are staging a hostile takeover of my common sense and ability to rationalize. They want me to reach down and shove Abe's left hand up just a little further until it's touching that needy little spot that only ever gets attention from my Finger Fun vibrator. His thick fingers would be a much better replacement, or even better, his tongue...

Abe's eyes finally reopen, looking even darker than before as they zero in on my lips. His right hand comes up and grabs a strand of my hair from my shoulder that makes my breath catch. I'm certain that he's about to kiss me when the sound of an approaching car in the once empty rest area interrupts. Abe and I both freeze like we were doing something naughty when, to the passerby, it only looks like we're having a casual conversation.

Disappointment hits like a bowling ball in my gut at the interruption since now I won't find out what Abe would've done if they hadn't pulled up and parked three spots away from us. Would he have kissed me? If so, would it have been light and soft or rough and dirty like how the man looks?

"It's time to take you home," Abe grumbles before he withdraws both of his hands and turns around to grab his helmet from the handlebar. He sounds angry and his movements are jerky as he secures the chin strap and then climbs back on the bike.

I guess that means our flirty banter is over.

Such a shame too. I wasn't ready for him to give up quite so soon.

CHAPTER FOUR

Abe

RIDING AROUND ON A HARLEY WITH A HARD-ON REALLY fucking sucks.

I don't remember the last time I was this damn horny. I mean, sure, I wake up with morning wood seeking a warm mouth like any other bastard, but never at this level of desperation.

It's so bad that I want to tug my zipper down just to let some of the pressure off. And my hard cock doesn't improve a bit on the way to Mercy's house. How could it with her arms around my waist, full breasts pressed to my back and thighs squeezing my waist? Not to mention that her hand is totally caressing my abs. Sure, she's trying to be discreet with her tiny movements, but I feel every single one of them.

Mercy yells out directional turns to me when we slow down and get into her neighborhood. A moment later we're at her house. I slow my bike down to pull into the driveway and try to keep myself in check as I park behind her silver BMW that Sasha brought over.

Right now, I'm a hair-trigger away from throwing her on the

ground and jerking the skirt of her dress up so I can see her pussy. Seeing it wouldn't be enough, though. I'd want to touch it and taste it, which would get me arrested if I do it in her front yard. On the other hand, she doesn't have many neighbors...

No, no, hell no, I tell my dick. We have to have a woman's permission before we start lifting skirts, and Mercy specifically told me that I didn't have a chance of getting in her panties. So he'll just have to wait for me to get back to my apartment at the clubhouse and find someone else to relieve the pressure.

My balls tighten as if to say *fuck that, it's Mercy or your hand, buddy.* The fantasy of her is gonna be ten times better than the real thing with anyone else. Likely for the rest of my miserable existence. Sad but true.

I kill the engine and sit back once Mercy climbs off the left side, staying seated on my bike, ready to get the fuck out of here before I attack her.

"Thanks for the ride," the gorgeous woman says sweetly from beside me as she smooths out the front of her blue dress.

"Welcome," I mutter, trying not to look directly at her for fear my inner caveman will come out. Instead, I look straight ahead and watch her from the corner of my eye.

Her heels click and clack on the concrete driveway as she starts to walk toward the front door of her house; but then she suddenly stops to dig into her purse, probably looking for her keys.

When Mercy remembers that Sasha and Chase used them to bring her car back, she goes over and opens the door; then bends down, I assume to retrieve them, giving me a great view of the curve of her ass. The fact that she doesn't have any panty lines means that she must be wearing a thong, the thought of which actually makes my cock cry a few tears. I knew the woman was out of my league, so I'm not surprised that she turned me down. What do I have to offer a classy woman like Mercy?

Finally finding her keys, Mercy straightens and shuts the driver door. I wait for her to head for the house, but instead she turns back toward me and click-clacks over. When she's standing next to me, she lets out a heavy sigh and then reaches over to...stick a coin down into my front jean pocket.

What the fuck?

Is she paying me for giving her a ride? If so, that's ridiculous, and the small piece of change is offensive.

I ease up my white-knuckled grip on the handlebars to retrieve the measly...dime so that I can give it back to her along with some serious attitude when Mercy says, "I've never done this before, and I can't promise that you won't regret it."

I want to say regret what, but my cock shushes me and tells me to look down at my shirt. Since I just grab the first tee in the clean pile every day, I don't usually notice the one I have on unless one of my brothers laughs at it or says something about it. That's why it takes me so damn long to remember that I'm wearing the "Beard Rides ten cents" one, and Mercy here just gave me...ten fucking cents.

There's no way in hell. Surely, I'm misunderstanding her. Or dreaming. But then I recall the last words she spoke, something about never doing this before and regret...and it hits me that she must mean that she doesn't want me to make her regret letting me put my tongue in her pussy.

Holy fuck.

"Or not. That's...that's probably for the best," Mercy says softly when I take too damn long to get off my bike. Hell, if I could rewind time back thirty seconds, I would already be inside her house with my face between her legs.

Trying to play my fuck-up cool, I tell her, "Get inside and get naked for me. Leave nothing on except your panties." The clipped words come out lower and harsher than I intended; but if she doesn't get moving soon, I'll eat her out right here in the front yard before God and everyone else.

Rather than look offended, Mercy nearly stumbles in her urgency to get to her front door.

If I had to guess, the odds are fifty-fifty for whether she goes inside and locks the door to keep me out or leaves it open in invitation. Okay, so maybe I'm being a little too optimistic. My odds are probably more like ninety-ten. Still, as soon as she unlocks the door and disappears inside, I intend to climb off my bike and find the fuck out.

If that door is open, then I've just become the luckiest son of a bitch in the world; and I won't waste the opportunity to make this gorgeous woman scream my name.

...

Mercy

OH MY, god! What the hell was I thinking? Did I really just *pay* a man for oral sex? I've never done anything like this before, so why would I up and decide that having a one-night stand now with a stranger is a good idea? It's definitely not. In fact, I'm sure that, as soon as my hormones settle down, I'll feel like a dirty little slut. Then, I'll be ashamed of how disappointing it was for Abe...

This is all Sasha's fault.

As I went to reach for my keys that Sasha left under the driver side floor mat like we used to do for each other back in college, there, lying in the middle of the black leather driver seat cushion was a shiny, new dime. I took it to be a sign that I should invite Abe in despite having a broken heart and getting ready for the *Queen of Hearts* to kick off later this week.

My hormones were yelling that tons of people have casual sex and that Sasha and I were the only ones in college who didn't. In a few days, I could potentially find Mr. Right, but what if Blake was right and I suck at sex or he's great in every category except for sex? I would love him anyway, but I don't want to miss out on seeing what all the fuss is about with wild, hot sex. If such a thing exists. Because looking at Abe, I'm fairly certain it'll be hot, at least for me. Hell, I'm more aroused as I step into my house, toss my purse on the floor and start peeling off my heels than I've probably ever been with a man, and he's barely touched me with more than the side of his thumb on my thigh. How will I react when his face is between my legs like I asked of him when I gave him that stupid dime?

A quick glance out the living room window shows Abe climbing off his bike and starting this way. Since he declared that I get naked except for my panties like he had all of the authority to do so and that there would be hell to pay if I don't comply, I jerk my dress over my head and toss it aside to start unclasping my bra. It's loose with the straps falling down my arm a second later.

Crap! Now what? He said to get naked, but he didn't say if he wanted me on the bed or...or in the living room.

What if I am horribly bad at sex and that's why it's never been any good with the few men I've slept with?

The front door creaks open behind me and then bangs shut hard, causing me to instinctively wrap one arm around my breasts and one over my panties to hide myself as I stand there in the middle of my entryway naked except for the sky-blue thong.

"Lord. Have. Mercy." Abe growls each word from behind me, sounding more like a feral beast than a man. Just his deep voice causes cold chill bumps to break out down my arms and legs. "Turn around," he orders, and I do so slowly, feeling completely out of my element but obligated to follow his commands. Besides, I'm too turned on to call this off now. If I tell him to leave, then I'll always wonder what I was missing. Still, it's hard to meet his eyes while standing so vulnerable before such a big man, but eventually I do. They're dark, bottomless pits of hunger.

Abe stalks toward me like a confident predator about to attack its prey. When his fully clothed body, smelling strongly of leather, nearly brushes the hairs on my arm covering my body, he drops down to his knees on the floor, putting him face level with my belly button because he's so damn tall. His big hands remain spread on the tops of his thighs so that the tip of his nose is the only part of him that touches me at first while I continue to cover myself. His eyes are closed tight as he runs his nose over the sensitive skin of my stomach, inhaling deeply as he goes and making me gasp as my core tightens and warms. My knees start to feel weak, so I try to keep them locked while the hungry wolf smells my skin. Lower and lower his nose goes until his face is pushing my hand away from where it's crossed over my lower body. I let it drop back to my side, revealing my panties to him.

When his nose rubs against my clit through the damp fabric, the words, "Oh, god!" burst free from my lips. Abe growls in response, which I take to mean that he approves. It's hard to know being in this particularly intimate position. His nose dips lower and wiggles back and forth between my thighs to try and make room, so I open my stance a little more to allow him entry. I feel Abe's hot breath of air heat up my panties when he exhales, then buries his face between my legs.

That's when I realize that my entire body is trembling slightly from the anticipation of what he'll do next and needing more. But I don't make a sound as he continues his exploration. Not until I feel the flat of his tongue press against the crotch of my panties and work its way up to the waistline, making me cry out from all the sensations – the wetness of his tongue, the tickling of his beard behind it. It's all too much, yet not enough.

When my eyes reopen, I look down and find Abe's dark gaze on mine before his teeth bite into the waist of my thong and he starts tugging the material down my legs as he watches my face. Around my calves, his teeth release the panties; and they fall to the floor on their own. Then, Abe's face is back to rubbing against my trimmed curls like a cat.

"I knew it," he says, his voice so low it's not much more than a mumble. "Love red pussy," he adds before the tip of his tongue flicks rapidly over the flesh between my legs.

"Ohgodohgod," I moan as my head falls back and my entire body shudders.

"Now you're gonna sit on my face," Abe says between presses of his lips up my pelvis and stomach. "And I'm gonna eat this pretty, red pussy until you beg me to stop. But I won't, not until you tell me the safe words."

Abe is lowering himself to the hardwood floor so that he's on his back with his head between my legs before I'm capable of forming a sentence.

"Wh-what are the, um, the safe words?" I stammer before I let out a screech when his enormous hands wrap around my shaking thighs and pull me down to the ground so that I'm straddling his face.

"You'll have to guess them," he says as his palms clamp down on the front of my thighs and his tongue starts to go into full-blown tornado mode in my pussy. My orgasm hits me with the intensity of a head-on collision, causing my hips to buck so hard that my upper body falls forward. My palms slap against Abe's hard stomach to catch myself while I chant his name over and over again.

It's like the waves of pleasure are never-ending. I lose track of how many times I come and what time it is. Hell, I couldn't even tell you what day it is. I'm a mindless, needy creature with one master and his name is...

"Abe! Abe, please," I tell the man who has taken control of my body while I clutch two-handfuls of his shirt in my fists. "I can't...I can't take any more." One of his thick fingers penetrates my tight, still clenching pussy, and my hips automatically start to grind down on it.

"I think you can handle a few more," is Abe's gruff response before his mouth is too busy sucking and licking on my clit for him to speak.

"Oh, fuuuck," I moan as my head falls forward, loving his tongue, especially with the addition of his finger inside of me, more than I should for a man I just met. Okay, so I'll let him make me come one more time and then I'll stop.

Three orgasms later...

Sweat is dripping down my neck and back, between my breasts. I've been burning up and shaking for so long I've forgotten what my life was like before Abe's tongue.

"Please...please...stop," I beg him through pants. "I need...I need..."

"Need what, Red. What do you need?" Abe grumbles from underneath my pussy.

"I need your cock inside of me right now!" I tell him, blurting out the words without thinking.

It must've been the right thing to say, because I'm rewarded with a swift smack of his palm on my ass.

"That's what I was waiting to hear," Abe confirms as his hand feels around to find the button of his jeans to pop it, since he can't see much with me still sitting on his face. The enormous bulge behind the zipper means he has to go slow as he tugs it down. There is no underwear in the way, so when he pushes his jeans down just a little lower on his hips, his mammoth cock pops free.

Jesus. Christ.

My eyes bulge as I try to take in all the veiny inches. I mean, I knew he'd be large but not King Kong size.

"Sorry, big guy, but, um, that's not gonna fit," I tell him with a shake of my head. I may be completely blissed out but I'm not delusional.

"You don't think so?" Abe asks as his hand wraps around the base of his cock.

"I know so!" I assure him.

"You're wet enough that I think you could take this foot long."

I bark out a laugh and say, "It's not the length I'm worried about. It's the...girth."

"I really want to try," Abe groans. "Sit on my cock and let me just get the tip wet."

Just the tip? That doesn't sound too terrible.

"Okay, just the tip," I warn him as I start to crawl down his body.

"I love this ass, but turn around so that I can see your face," he tells me with another slap to one of my ass cheeks.

"Yes, sir," I agree, a slave to anything he asks of me after giving me more orgasms than I could count. No man has ever done that to me, or even gone down on me. Blake and the few other men I've dated always treated me like I was a fragile doll that they couldn't touch for too long or I might break. Which means they fucked me fast, missionary style and that was that.

My limbs are so clumsy that it takes me a minute to finally get turned around to face Abe as I lower my hips down on his... "Wow," I moan as my dripping wet slit comes into contact with the length of his hard, velvety flesh.

"Damn, that's nice," Abe groans as he reaches down to wrangle his python so that the blunt tip is pressed to my entrance. My walls easily expand to accommodate his thickness.

"Oh, fuck, Mercy!" he shouts, holding my hips tightly while he thrusts upward to pump just a few more inches inside of me before retreating. "Ride me a little, Red. Whatever you can take," he pleads, sounding like he's in pain. I want to give him some relief like he gave me, so I grind down on him and then bounce back up once...twice... and by the third time he's as deep as he can go.

My eyes widen and my lips part on a surprised gasp as I stay seated on his cock while looking down at Abe's face. His eyelids are so low they're barely open more than a slit, but I know he's looking at me.

"You like that? Me stretching you the way no one else has before?" he grits out through his clenched jaw.

"Yes," I reply in a whisper since it's impossible for me to move when I'm completely impaled on him.

"Play with yourself," he orders, and my fingertips gladly comply, reaching down with my right hand to rub two of them on my clit while my left hand is braced on Abe's chest that's rising and falling rapidly. My eyes shut tight as I focus on my fingertips and his fullness.

The hands gripping my hips move around to squeeze each of my ass cheeks before they hold them down right as Abe pumps his hips upward.

"Oh, shit!" I exclaim at the intensity of the head of his cock hitting what feels like a very full, very heavy water balloon inside of me.

"Keep touching yourself," he commands as he continues to thrust upward faster and faster while I try to hang on for the ride. "That's it," Abe encourages me when my fingers get back to work on my clit. "Have to pull out soon," he tells me through panting breaths.

"Don't you dare stop!" I warn him as I start slamming myself down on his cock with each of his upward thrusts. "I'm too close. Fuck me, big guy, or I'll never let you touch me again!"

The wet slapping sound of our bodies and our moans grow louder as we both move faster.

"After you come, I'm gonna lick the sweat from your titties," he tells me.

"Yes!" I cry out as I get closer and closer to popping that balloon inside of me. So close, just need to hit it a little harder. A little faster. "YES!" I exclaim when it bursts, and then I'm lost to the flood of euphoric waves.

CHAPTER FIVE

Abe

"HOLY FUCK!" I GROAN WHEN MERCY'S HOT LITTLE PUSSY starts clenching around my cock. Nothing has ever felt so tight and wet and fucking amazing as this.

My entire body seizes up like I'm having one massive muscle cramp, and then it happens — I bust a load inside of her that's no smaller than that of a small lake. But her pussy doesn't let me go until I give up every last drop of cum I have in my reserves, making sure I'm too empty to ever fuck anyone else again. I'll gladly give up every ounce of liquid in my body for her if it makes her happy.

"So good," I hear Mercy murmuring over and over again from above me as she keeps riding my now withering cock like she has no clue he's called it quits for the rest of my life.

I'm too exhausted to even tell her I've already finished...

Oh fuck. That realization makes my after-fuck high fizzle right out.

I came *inside* of her like a fucking idiot.

Oh, shit. Oh, shit!

"Birth control?" I blurt out, but Mercy just looks at me with a content grin on her face, her eyelids losing the fight to stay open before she collapses onto my chest and makes happy "mmm" sounds while I'm freaking the fuck out.

Needing to know the answer to this question now, I peel the sexy, sweaty woman off of me and lay her gently on the hard floor so that I can get to my feet. My first stop is to retrieve her purse that she dropped around the door when she came in and undressed for me. Normally I wouldn't go digging through a woman's shit, but desperate times call for desperate measures. I zip it open and dig around but don't see one of those fucking plastic pill containers. Fuck!

Where else could it be? Bathroom maybe?

I wander around the house bouncing off walls in the hallway while I look for the bathroom since my blood is still working its way back up into my brain.

When I find it, I open the cabinet doors but don't find any pills in there either.

Okay, so kitchen? Some people have meds in there since they need a drink of water to wash them down.

It's my next stop. I flip open all the top cabinets and bottom ones but it's just pots, pans, plates and bowls.

"Motherfucker," I mutter aloud.

"What are you lookin' for, big guy?" Mercy asks, words slurring as she calls out to me from the living room. When I come out of the kitchen and see her lying naked on her stomach on the living room floor with the side of her face resting happily on her crossed arms, red hair puddling around her like a goddess who fell from the sky, I almost decide it would be worth it to knock her up and make her mine.

Shaking that idiotic thought from my head, I answer her. "Your birth control pills."

"Mmm," she replies, then, "You won't find any."

Oh fuck. The blood that was once returning to my head suddenly drains again.

Mercy tilts her head to look over at me and then giggles. "Don't worry. I'm on the shot."

When I just blink at her in confusion as to what that means, she finally says, "The birth control shot. Kids would ruin my career."

"Oh, thank god," I gasp before my legs give out with relief and I take a seat right against the living room wall. "I never want kids. That's why I always use condoms and never come inside bitches," I grumble in agreement as I rub my palm down my face to wipe away the sweat.

"Excuse me?" Mercy asks, the indignation in her voice obvious.

Rethinking my words, I say, "I never come inside of...beautiful women. You're the first."

"Aw, that's so sweet and a little sad for you," she replies. "Condoms suck. But how do you find any big enough to cover King Kong?"

"King Kong?" I repeat, followed by a chuckle at her naming my cock. "I have to use rubber gloves," I joke.

"I don't doubt it," Mercy says. Rolling to her back, she lifts her knees and stretches her arms over her head. Releasing a breathy, "Wow," she goes on to say, "That was even better than I expected. Sasha is the best friend in the world. I'm gonna send her flowers tomorrow to thank her for introducing us."

Tipping her head back to see me, she says, "I definitely got my money's worth out of that dime."

Reaching inside my pants, I find the dime that I put away before I came inside and know it's one I won't ever spend.

Fucking Mercy was so damn amazing. I just hope I can trust her, because I don't want any kids or an old lady. That's a whole lot of responsibility that could land in my lap all because I was too damn caught up in the moment, in the feel of her tight, wet pussy to stop and put on a rubber.

Finally, Mercy sits up and starts gathering her clothes and shoes while I watch, enjoying the sight of her naked body bending over. I thought my cock was done for the day, or hell, the rest of my life after the amazing way she used it, but he gives an appreciative twitch like he could probably make it happen again. I haven't even zipped my pants yet but was apparently running around Mercy's house with my dick flopping around as I looked for pills that don't exist. While I'm still pissed at myself for my momentary lapse in judgment, I don't put King Kong away just yet either...

"So, um, thanks for...that," Mercy says. "I hope it was okay for you..."

"Yeah, ah, no problem," I tell her, not used to having women thank me for fucking them like it was a chore or some shit.

She has all of her clothing clutched to the front of her body, hiding her tits and gorgeous, red pussy from me. I didn't really get a chance to bury my face in those titties or suck on them like I would like to, and she's dismissing me. What else did I expect? I'm one lucky son of a bitch because the classy woman let me touch her in the first place. I never expected her to let me eat her out or fuck her, but I know it was a one-time thing. Done and over. Too damn bad.

"I need to, um, go clean up in the bathroom," she informs me with red coloring her cheeks, and I nearly groan thinking about my cum running down her thighs. Fuck, I wish I could see that.

When Mercy continues to stand stock-still, I eventually realize that she wants me to get the hell out of her house.

"Oh, right, I'll get going," I agree as I get to my feet and reluctantly tuck my semi-hard cock back into my jeans to zip up. "I'll just lock the door on the way out," I tell her.

"Okay, thanks, Abe," Mercy says before she scurries off down the hall and I hear a door shut, signaling the end of my time in the gorgeous woman's presence.

Am I disappointed that it's over? Hell yes, because I would've loved to come inside of her a few more times even if it's incredibly stupid. But I didn't expect anything more. Fuck, I was lucky just to be able to get inside of her once. And usually, I prefer when the club sluts get dressed and leave my room right after we finish fucking. I mean, I'll keep my mouth shut if they decide to stick around, but only because I don't want to be an asshole. Getting off is all I really care about though with any woman.

So then why does it feel like my boots are filled with cement when I try to make my feet leave Mercy's house? And why the fuck does it feel like I'm leaving something behind when I finally make myself lock her front door and pull it closed behind me?

CHAPTER SIX

Mercy

As soon as I step out of the shower, I hear the faint sound of my phone ringing from my purse that's still in the living room.

And I know it has to be either Sasha or my mother. My mother will worry if she calls and I don't answer, so I wring out as much water as I can from my long hair and wrap my towel around me to go answer.

Droplets of water leak down onto my purse as I dig around for my phone and finally find it.

"Hi, Mom," I answer after seeing her name on the screen. Then, I take a seat right there on the floor instead of sitting on my new microfiber sofa and getting it wet, just a few feet away from where I did the nasty with a man I just met.

"What were you doing? You sound out of breath," my mother says in a rush.

"I just got out of the shower."

"Why were you showering in the middle of the afternoon?" she asks.

Jeez, my mother is like a crazy, mad dog detective on one of those crime shows.

"It's a hot, muggy day and I wanted to cool off," I explain, leaving off the part about how my body was dripping sweat and other bodily fluids, not entirely my own, from the dirty floor sex. I would even question whether or not the unbelievably good fucking actually happened to me if not for the soreness between my legs from being impaled on the biggest dick I've ever seen. That's all the proof I need that I really had a one-night stand.

I wait for the guilt and self-loathing to surface after doing something so crazy and out of character, but as of right now they're still absent. Guess the endorphins haven't worn off yet. Any time now I'll be regretting my decision and wishing I could go back in time and stick the dime in my purse rather than in Abe's pocket like he was a giant, walking, talking orgasm vending machine. Did he enjoy himself? I mean, I know he came inside of me, but that doesn't mean it was necessarily good sex, right? It could've just been boring sex for him.

"Do you have a fever?" my mother asks. "Is that why you're hot?"

"No, Mom," I reply with a roll of my eyes. "I'm perfectly heathy."

"Are you getting plenty of sleep? You need to be well rested to get rid of the bags under your eyes before the photo shoot."

"I'm sleeping at least eight hours a night," I assure her. "And I don't have bags under my eyes."

"Are you sure? I want you to put your best foot forward with the bachelors," my mother says. "You're running out of time. If you don't get married before you're thirty, then you may as well forget having kids. And you want kids, don't you?"

"I have plenty of time," I disagree as I stretch out on my back on the floor. "Who says women have to marry before thirty to have kids?"

"That's just how it works."

"Uh-huh," I say to humor her.

"Now, the first men you need to get rid of on the show are the most handsome ones," she tells me. "If a man is too handsome, he'll cheat on you, just like your father did to me. So pick someone who isn't classically handsome but not awful to look at."

"So you're saying that all handsome men are cheaters?" I challenge.

"Yes!" she exclaims. "They won't ever stop looking for someone better. And when they find it, they'll leave you alone to raise their kids while they start a new family."

My poor mother. When I was six, my father moved out of the house. He divorced her, remarried, and forgot that the two of us ever existed. According to my mother's gossiping friends down in Florida where my father lives, I have a half-brother and half-sister out in the world that I've never met. It's a tough pill to swallow thinking that he didn't give a shit about me but loves his other children enough to stick around. But I can't imagine how hard it's been on my mother losing the man she loved to another woman after they had started a family together. It was brutal finding out Blake wanted someone else, and we had only been dating a few weeks. How hard must it be to devote your life and love to a man and have him trample all over it like it's nothing but dog shit on his shoes?

"Are you listening to me, Mercy? Don't pick the handsome men. Keep the ugly ones around and see if any of them attend church regularly. If not, then you should finally go out with Joseph. He never misses a single Wednesday bible study or Sunday school."

"I don't think there are many single men out in the world who attend church other than Joseph," I point out, cringing at the reminder of the dumpy, excessively sweaty man my mom always makes me talk to before we can leave the parking lot on Sundays. Not that I'm very spiritual myself. The only reason I go to church is because my mother guilt trips me into it. When we were traveling, she dragged me to some type of service every single, bright and early, Sunday morning.

Then, she would spend the rest of the day complaining about how wrong they did everything that wasn't exactly like her small, strict, uber-conservative Baptist church that she was raised in.

"Well, more single men should come to church! That's what's wrong with the world. People don't talk to Jesus anymore. They sin too much and don't never even bother to ask forgiveness!"

The reminder of how I sinned this afternoon causes a blush to creep up my neck and cheeks. My mother thinks I'm a virgin, which is insane. Even if she thought I hadn't had premarital sex before the show, she should've figured it out by now. If she found out that I had slept with a man I just met, a tatted biker at that, she'd probably be on my doorstep with the preacher, ready to exorcise the demons he left in my body.

"You're staying on the path of the righteous, aren't you, Mercy?" my Mom asks, which is, of course, when that guilt and self-loathing tries to rear its ugly head.

"Yes, mother," I reply so that she won't worry about me burning in hell when I die.

"You're such a good girl," she says. "And some men still prefer good girls over those loose ones."

"I bet you're right," I tell her as I close my eyes and grit my teeth to get through the rest of this phone call. "I need to go dry my hair before I get pneumonia," I say to get her off the phone.

"You should. And take your temperature afterward to make sure you're not running a fever," she tells me.

"I will. Love you, Mom," I say.

"Love you too, Mercy. I better see you at early service tomorrow! Don't make your poor mother sit in the pew all pitiful and alone, Mercy Grace Daniels!" she replies before I end the call.

Sasha has never understood why I tolerate my mother's craziness, but she wouldn't understand since both of her parents are still happily married. After my father left us, I'm all that my mom has left other than her handful of elderly church friends who haven't kicked the bucket yet. So, I put up with her judgment, ancient advice, and sermons to make her happy and think that I'm following all of her old school wisdom.

And yeah, it's exhausting to pretend like I'm a good girl.

...

Abe

MY HEAD WAS all over the place after I left Mercy's house, still thinking about the mistake I made by not using a condom, while having a hard time regretting it. Sure, it felt fucking amazing to be inside of the first pussy ever without a barrier, but the consequences aren't worth a few minutes of ecstasy.

So then why is it every time that I run through the memories, I wouldn't do a damn thing differently except beg to stay for a few minutes longer.

When it starts to get dark, I leave the same pier as the restaurant where the mob of people with cameras were after Mercy and head back to the clubhouse. Tonight, the Kings are gonna bang some heads together at the Aces' bar, so I need to get over the shit that happened this afternoon and get ready.

That's the only reason why I turn down Cynthia's offer to come downstairs with me. Right?

Or maybe it's because I still taste and smell Mercy's mango scent on me and don't want anyone fucking that up just yet.

"You're here early," Chase says when he walks into the chapel and sees me already sitting in my chair.

"Ready to get this done," I tell him as he takes his seat next to me and leaves the chair at the head of the table empty for Torin.

"How did things go with Mercy?" he asks, holding out his palm for my cell phone to put in the bucket that always stays outside the room during our meetings.

"Fine," I mutter as I pull the device from my pocket and hand it to him.

"Fine?" Chase repeats. "That's it. Just fine? You were pussy-whipped before you found out her name," he adds with a chuckle.

"No, I wasn't," I declare.

"I thought you were gonna drag her out of the restaurant by her hair," Chase jokes. "And I think that's what Sasha was betting on when she asked us to show up."

"What do you mean?" I ask.

"My old lady was obviously pimping you out," he replies with a smirk. "So, did you show her best friend a good time or not?"

"Yeah, we had a good time," I agree.

"No shit?" Chase mutters. "Sasha said you would, but no offense, I didn't think you had a chance with Mercy."

"I didn't either," I agree. Then, surprising even myself, I tell him, "I want more."

"Hell, we're men. We always want more," he replies.

"No, I mean, I want to see her again," I explain.

"You sure about that?" Chase asks. "Sasha says the girl has a ton of baggage. Why don't you just forget her and find Cynthia when we get back tonight? Less complicated."

"Right," I agree, even though I don't want Cynthia or anyone else. I just want to go back to Mercy's house and crawl into bed with her tonight. Nah, that's too pathetic. Maybe I could buy her some flowers or some other shit and go by tomorrow. I mean, not to be a pussy or whatever, but should I keep an eye on her in case she was wrong about the shot thing and I knocked her up? If so, I want to be the first to know that shit. They make those Plan B pills for fuck-ups like mine. If I got her one of those, would she take it just to be absolutely sure?

One by one, our brothers start wandering in, dropping off their phones and taking their seats at the table. I wasn't sure who all would be involved in our assault tonight, but it looks like everyone is here... except for Dalton.

Could he be our rat? Doubtful since he's been around the MC almost as long as Chase has. His father was a founding member of the Savage Kings and Dalton now handles our dirty money, funneling it through the legit businesses to cover our asses. It wouldn't make sense for him to fuck us over.

The door opens and in walks the blond bastard. "Fuck. Sorry I'm late," Dalton says, sounding out of breath. "Cynthia was insistent, and you know how good her mouth is," he adds with a grin in my direction before he shoots his phone into the bucket like it's a basketball.

And yeah, I do know, but I'm not the least bit jealous that, when I turned the redhead down, she approached Dalton, the biggest manwhore of us all. We share her, like most of the other girls upstairs. Then, I try to think about how I would feel if one of the guys touched Mercy, and I can feel the vein in my head throbbing in rage at just the idea.

Even more surprising than Dalton coming is late is when the door opens again and Torin comes in. While he hasn't shaved his thick, dirty-blond beard, he at least looks cleaner, missing the sand that was covering nearly every inch of him earlier.

"Glad you made it," Chase says before everyone else welcomes him back. It's been weeks since he's even stepped foot in the building.

"Let's do this," he says before he takes a seat on the floor with his back against the wall and knees raised, refusing to sit in his chair at the head of the table.

Chase looks slightly disappointed but shakes it off when he places the phone bucket outside the door and shuts it. Torin's the only member Chase doesn't ask to pony up his phone since it's not like he's the rat, and I'm guessing he doesn't want to rock the boat by asking for it.

Addressing the rest of the table, Chase says, "Sorry to call everyone in so late, but we need a full table tonight. You all know that Hector Cruz and his crew skipped town after...what happened." Chase pauses, glancing over at Torin to make sure he's holding it together. When Torin gives a slight nod, Chase continues. "Reece has been doing everything he can to try to track him down."

Reece leans forward and raps his knuckles on the table; then waits for Chase to acknowledge him. "These Cartel guys are spooks," Reece says. "When they draw too much attention to themselves, they fade away; then pop up with a new identity in another part of the country. I'm using every trick I know to get a hit on Hector or one of his associates, but it's a slow process. I talked to Chase about it, and we thought that this situation might call for a more direct approach."

"We know that these Cartel cunts approached the Ace of Spades MC," Chase continues. "They were using them as distributors in our town. Abe and I put a stop to that shit. But with the recent events, I think it would be a good idea to revisit their clubhouse and express how unhappy we are with their choice of business partners."

"We're going to burn that fucking place to the ground," Torin declares.

Every one of my brothers slap the table in agreement and roar in approval before Chase raises a hand for silence. "We're gonna burn that fucking place to the ground," he agrees. "But first we're gonna ask some questions. Here's how this is gonna go down, and even more reason why we have to do it tonight. Reece has been keeping an eye on the Aces and has found out that they still have a functioning meth lab in a trailer they've been moving around. That trailer is parked at their bar right now."

"Meth labs blow up all the time," Sax laughs, before a glare from Chase shuts him up.

"Yeah, that's kind of the point," Chase sighs. "Now, we also know that four of their members rode south earlier today. Reece pinged them at a gas station in Florida this evening, so they're not coming home tonight. Finally, we got a call from Jade just giving us a heads-up that the local police are setting up a big ass check-point on both ends of the strand late tonight, looking for drunks. They will be at least fifteen minutes away when any calls come in about the hell we're going to raise out at the Aces' bar. Here's what I need from each one of you."

As Chase lays out the plan for our raid tonight, I'm finally able to push Mercy to the back of my mind. I know she'll come storming back as soon as I have some quiet time, but right now I've got work for my fists and brains, not my cock and heart.

Once all of my brothers have confirmed they know their roles, Chase points to the wall clock.

"It's almost midnight now," he tells us. "Grab what you will need, get a drink, and be ready to ride at one. I want to be at their bar right after closing." Casting one more worried glance at Torin, Chase picks up the gavel and slams it down.

Most of my brothers jump to their feet in excitement, then pause to watch as Torin storms out of the chapel. As the rest of us begin to file out, I hear Chase tell War, the sergeant-at-arms, "Stay by him, man. Don't let him get himself killed tonight or do anything else stupid."

"That's what I've been doing for years," War grumbles good-naturedly. "I'll stay close to Torin, just like we planned. You keep Abe with you, and everything will work out fine. This is going to be good for us, brother. I'm proud of you."

I see Chase slap War on the back before I start down the hall towards my room. Chase detailed my part in tonight's activities for everyone else to hear, but he never had to explain it to me. I stand by him, wherever we go, just the way it's always been since I was a prospect and he was my sponsor.

Out in the hallway, Gabriel stops me with a raised hand, bringing me up short. Things are always awkward with my little brother, and my head's not in a good place for a heart-to-heart with him right now. "What's up?" I ask him.

"Did you tell Chase to leave me at the clubhouse with Fast Eddie and Reece? Come on, man, you don't have to pull this big brother shit on me with the MC. You guys can use me out there tonight." Gabe says, low enough so that everyone in the hall doesn't overhear.

"You know I don't tell Chase how to do a goddamned thing," I reply shortly. I almost add that, if he had asked, I *would* have told him to keep my little brother out of harm's way. But for once, I manage to grit my teeth before my first thought falls out of my mouth. "Think about our last run," I add, to console him. "We left Reece here with just the prospects, and the place got torn up. If Chase wants you here, it's because he trusts you to hold down the fort."

Gabe nods, thankfully accepting the reasoning. "Yeah, when you put it that way, it makes more sense." Raising his hand for a fist bump, I hit his knuckles and we share a grin. "You know I've been meaning to talk to you..." he starts to add, before I cut him off.

"Later, wild man. I've got to get ready."

"All right, Abe, I hear you," Gabe says with a sigh, before turning to head upstairs.

Once I'm back in my room, I start digging my gear out of my closet. I debate taking a few minutes to go to one of the clubs' computers and run a quick search on Mercy, maybe find out more about her or just see some pictures, but I quickly dismiss that notion. Chase didn't give any of us our phones back after the meeting. Most of the brothers don't know, but he's still worried about a rat among us. If anyone is seen making a call, or anyone besides Reece is on a computer, it will draw attention. I don't need these guys riding my ass about my ravishing redhead while we've got work to do.

I take off my cut and hang it up for tonight, replacing it with an unadorned leather riding vest. It looks plain, but it's anything but ordinary. All of my brothers have one just like it, lined with Kevlar and reinforced polymer plates. I rack the pump on my shotgun, fill the tube with shells, and then place half a dozen more in the loops on the carrying strap before throwing it over my shoulder. After I check my pistol and slide two more clips into the holster on my hip, I'm ready to ride.

When I stomp up the stairs to the bar, I can see immediately that Torin or Chase already cleared everyone out. The only people here are my brothers, with the two prospects behind the bar serving the drinks. I lean on the bar beside Chase and motion for Holden to pour me a tall one.

"You been keeping an eye on everyone?" I lean over and say quietly to Chase.

"You're the only one that's been out of my line-of-sight since we were in the chapel," Chase assures me. "Don't give me that ugly look," he laughs, patting me on the back when I scowl at him.

"It's the only look I've got," I growl, before taking a long pull on the frosted mug Holden slides over to me.

"I wasn't hinting that I think you're...you know, the rat," Chase whispers. "I've never had any doubts about you, brother. Not once."

"Same," I reply, clinking my glass against the bottle he's holding. Nodding over to where Torin is sitting at the other end of the bar, I tell Chase, "Glad to see he's switched to soda tonight."

"That ain't soda," Chase grumbles as Torin crumples up a red Solo cup and tosses it towards the trash can. "He's drinking that damned *Evan Williams* that makes him get even more ornery than usual. He dropped a bottle earlier, so I told him he had to use sippy cups and ride in the van with the prospects."

I snort my beer when Chase tells me that, which sets him off cackling as I splutter and laugh. Torin's head snaps over, and he glares at us as he stomps around the bar. "You two jokers having fun tonight?" Torin demands. "The show's over, and I'm ready to get to the afterparty." Slapping each of our chests, he gives a satisfied grunt. "I checked the rest of them. Everybody's got their plates on. Let's go, Kings!" he roars as we all jump up and file out to our bikes.

Chase pulls his bike across the parking lot to make sure he's in the front of our convoy with the van bringing up the rear. Sticking to the back roads, we barely see any other vehicles on our ride over to the Aces' clubhouse. Torin has the prospect flash the van's lights to pull us all over when we're about a mile away and calls Reece. After he makes sure that any surveillance equipment is shut down, he gets us back on the road.

The Ace of Spades' clubhouse is a traditional pool hall, with a gravel parking lot. It's just after two a.m. when our crew roars onto the property, our bikes slinging rocks at the few vehicles still parked out front. Torin's been inside before, just like Chase and I have, so he has the prospect drive the van around to the back of the building. We've planned to have him lead War, Sax, and Dalton in that way.

I'm off my bike with my shotgun in my hands before the dust we kicked up has even started to settle. I run ahead of Chase, Cooper, and Miles, shoving one of the double glass doors open with my shoulder. Letting out an ear-splitting roar, I swing my shotgun around the corner of the small foyer leading into the main room, unloading a blast into the lines of bottles behind the bar. Glass explodes and rains down around a huge, bald guy that I recognize as the bartender who was here the last time Chase and I visited. He's got a pistol in his hand; and as he hops backwards, he fires a shot at me before he slips and falls on his ass.

I can't laugh at him, because the slug this bullseye motherfucker fired hits me square in the chest, blasting the wind from my lungs and staggering me backwards. Miles races past me, the AK-47 in his hands blinding me as it spits fire and brass across the room. I can see Torin and War at the back of the room, ushering club sluts out the back door as Chase helps me back to my feet.

"Abe, goddammit, how bad is it?" Chase yells at me, jerking on my damned beard to get me to look at him.

"Don't ever do that again," I wheeze as I lean on him for a moment. "The beard is sacred, man. Let's handle our business. I'm fine, bro. It didn't go through," I confirm, slapping my right side with a wince.

"Stay down, motherfucker!" Miles shouts as Chase leaves me to collect myself. I can see now that Miles has three dudes down on their knees, while War drags the bartender by the scruff of his cut around to join them.

Letting him go, War looks directly at me as the bartender gets to his knees. "All right, Abe?" War grunts.

"Yeah, Abe, how's that feel, you bleeding pussy?" the bartender snorts. "You think you're some kind of fucking hero, storming in here like Clint Eastwood or something?"

"I ain't no hero," I tell him, racking another round into my shotgun. "But I am a man that will take a bullet for what he loves. Can you say the same?" I ask him, levelling the barrel at his face.

"I can't believe I missed your fat fucking head..." the bartender snarls. Before he can say anything else, War's lips twist in a furious scowl, and he raises the .45 he's got gripped in one massive fist up high, before bringing it crashing down right on top of the big guy's bald head. His scalp explodes, and he collapses faster than if War had actually shot him.

With the girls gone and the exits covered, Torin stomps over to the other bikers sprawled out on the floor. Looking them over, he spits on the hardwood floor before dragging two of them to their feet by fistfuls of their hair.

"Fucking prospects," he hisses, looking at their cuts. "How old are you little shits?" Torin asks.

One of them is cross-eyed drunk, and just stares in awe at Torin towering over him, knowing that he is looking at the reaper made flesh. The other one seems to have his wits about him, and stammers, "Eighteen...sir, we're both eighteen! Please, we didn't....we don't..."

"Shut the fuck up!" Torin barks, slapping the kid across the face. "I'll give you three seconds to take off that cut and get the hell out of town. This charter of the Ace of Spades MC is getting decommissioned, you understand?"

"Yes, sir!" the scrawny little punk stammers, shedding his cut like it just caught fire. He rips the one off his friend too, throwing them both at the man still lying on the floor. "This ain't what you promised, Johnny," he whines, before he and his buddy start easing towards the back door.

"Take that pile of shit with you!" Torin yells, pointing at the bartender bleeding on the floor. The two former prospects both grab an ankle and, under War's watchful gaze and gun, begin dragging him out the back door.

While Torin was taking out the trash, Chase directed Sax and Dalton to pull the Ace of Spades' club president, Johnny Martin, to his feet. They each had one of his arms, but to Johnny's credit, he was standing tall with his head held high. "You still alive, Chase Fury?" he laughed. "Figured Hector Cruz would have done you in by now."

Before Chase can respond, Torin steps in front of him. Johnny pales when he stares into Torin's bloodshot eyes. "Hector fucking Cruz gunned down *my wife*, murdered *my son*, and you're going to stand there and *laugh?*" Torin screams into his face.

"I didn't have shit to do with that, Torin. You know we don't go after families..." Johnny starts.

"You had *everything* to do with it!" Torin screams, almost incomprehensible in his rage. "*You* made the deal that brought them here. *You* got in bed with the fucking Cartel, and *MY FAMILY DIED!*" Torin roars the last few words, and then grabs Johnny by his ponytail and slams his fist into his face repeatedly, punctuating his outrage.

"Now tell me," Torin gasps. "Where the fuck is Hector hiding? So help me Christ, if you say 'I don't know,' I'll make you eat your own cock."

Johnny sags down between Sax and Dalton, apparently defeated. Off balance, Sax staggers a bit, and Johnny flashes a grin as he rips his arm away from Sax and shoves him backwards, where he falls over a chair. Dalton tries to grab his other arm, but Johnny snatches the knife from Dalton's belt sheath, lashing out at Torin with it.

Torin quickly grabs for his own knife, but it's War who is the fastest. One of his huge arms shoves Torin back as Johnny lunges, plunging the knife into War's forearm. War jerks his arm away as Torin catches his balance then charges forward, slamming his knife into Johnny's guts.

"I...don't...know..." Johnny gasps, still grinning, at Torin.

With another scream, Torin rips the knife upward, staring wild-eyed into Johnny Martin's face as the blade finds his heart. Johnny collapses at his feet, as the rest of us stare in shock.

Sax staggers to his feet, looking at Torin and War in horror. "I'm sorry, man, he was heavier than he looked, and..."

"Shut up," War snaps, gingerly pulling Dalton's long knife out of his forearm. The blade went all the way through the wide, meaty area, and he draws it out clean with a scowl. Going around the bar, he finds a towel; and Dalton helps him tie it around the cut. "It's fine," War huffs at Dalton. "Eddie can stitch it up. Clean your knife and let's finish this."

Torin is still standing there, staring down at Johnny's body. Chase looks like he's about to put an arm around him, but instead waves to Sax. "You and Cooper take Torin outside and keep watch. Everyone else grab the cash or any souvenirs you might want while Abe and I get this place cooking. Miles, get to the trailer out back and get it rigged."

I'm already on my way to the kitchen behind the bar. Reece had checked the club's utilities, and we know they've got a natural gas stove. I've got my wind back now. And with my adrenaline up, pulling the oven away from the wall barely takes any effort. "I see the gas line," I call to Chase, who is in the main room spraying around bottles of liquor that I didn't destroy with my shotgun. "I'm poking a hole in it now. Tell Miles he can light up whatever he brought."

I run back into the main room to find that Miles is already back from lighting up the trailer out back. He has kicked Johnny's body over, and has jabbed a bunch of sparklers into the former Ace of Spades president's cut. With a huge, childlike grin, Miles lights them up, and we all rush outside to our bikes while Johnny begins to pop and spark cheerily.

Torin is just standing there stone-faced next to the van as we all mount up. "Get in the fucking van!" Chase roars at his brother. "If you stay here until it blows, it will come back on the MC. The cops will be here soon!"

With a startled jerk, Torin snaps back, giving Chase a nod before he finally jumps into the passenger seat. We all peel out of the lot as the first sparks of the fire that Miles set in the Aces' meth lab trailer flicker over the roof from behind the bar. We're less than a mile away when the foggy gloom of the late coastal night erupts in a plume of light behind us. All of us pull to the side of the road to watch the fireball erupt into the sky.

Dalton is the first to break the silence, as his howls of laughter suddenly trigger the joy that had been building inside all of us. We got out of there in one piece, and we put the final nail in the coffin of those fucking pricks who had tried to spread their filth in our town. The fire will destroy Johnny's body and any traces we may have left behind, but those who need to know will get the message. The Savage Kings are fucking true one-percenters, born in blood and fire.

We make it back to the clubhouse by three-thirty in the morning, all of us trudging in wearily to see Turtle, Fast Eddie and Gabe still hanging out at the bar. Eddie jumps up when he sees the blood dripping down War's arm, mumbling, "I'll get my kit," as he limps off to the storage closet.

"Get your asses behind the bar and take some orders," Chase barks to the prospects, as we all collapse into chairs around the bar. Holden and Maddox scuttle, passing out bottles and glasses.

I see Cynthia and another girl, whose name I can't remember, come out of the kitchen when they hear all the commotion a few minutes later. I stop at a table and take a moment to peel off my vest and t-shirt. When Cynthia sees the fist-sized bruise still spreading across my chest, she rushes over to me.

"Damn, Abe, what happened to you tonight?" she whispers, taking a seat at the table with me.

"What the hell are you doing here?" I ask her since Chase had cleared everyone out before we left.

"You know I can't stay away," she replies. "Now why the hell does your chest look like it's about to split open?"

I roll my vest over on the table, showing her the bullet embedded into the mesh. "Got shot," I say simply as her mouth falls open. "War got it a lot worse, though," I add, hoping to get her to go away. "Maybe you ought to go see if he...needs anything."

"Yeah, Abe, okay," Cynthia agrees, giving me a sad, little smile. For some reason, that look makes me feel like a fucking swine, and I gently take her hand before she can walk away.

"Hey, wait a second..." I pause, trying to get a grip on what the hell I'm feeling. It suddenly hits me, harder than that damned bullet from earlier. That look on her face, that feeling of rejection when you're putting yourself out there...that's how I felt when Mercy asked me to leave earlier. It was actually physically painful, almost nauseating, and I just did it to this poor girl.

"I've taken a lot of shit for granted," I begin, as her forehead wrinkles in confusion. "What I mean is, I've taken you for granted. I've always thought that you ladies were just here for a good time, you know, free drinks and easy rides. We used you, and you used us, you understand?" I ask her, as I struggle to express this new, foreign idea.

Cynthia sits down at the table with me again, nodding in understanding. "Abe, we know the score. We love you guys, your lifestyle, everything about the club. But you know, when two people get physical, the way we do, sometimes..."

"Yeah," I agree, "Sometimes it's not just fucking. If your partner is special, feelings get involved."

"They do," Cynthia nods, before staring at me with her heart in her eyes. "You're special to me, Abe."

"That's why I wanted to apologize," I say firmly as I lean across the table to her, getting close to make sure there are no more misunderstandings between us. "You and me, we were always just sex. You're amazing, but that's all this ever was. I just realized tonight that maybe, for you, it was more, and I wanted you to know that I'm sorry. I'm not gonna put you in that situation anymore, string you along or anything like that. I only recently realized how shitty it feels, and I'm not going to be the cause of that for anyone else."

Cynthia gives me another small smile, before standing up from the table. "Thanks, Abe, for being honest. I'll be around, you know, if you change your mind about things. And listen, try not to spend so much time in your own head, honey. Don't let that little bullet that hit you get you all twisted up," she tells me, flipping her long, red hair back over her shoulder, before she struts off back behind the bar.

I don't bother telling her that it wasn't the bullet that got in my head or under my skin. It was a few hours with the most beautiful woman I've ever met, and God help me, I need more Mercy.

The rest of my brothers are gathered around the bar where Fast Eddie has opened up an old, beat-up tackle box revealing an ambulance load of medical supplies. He's already popped on some latex gloves; and while War is taking pulls from a bottle of scotch, he's sticking needles into the big man's arm and getting the sutures ready. After watching for a few minutes, Torin, Chase, and my little brother Gabe break away and all head towards the table where I'm sitting.

"You need anything, Abe?" Chase asks me as Torin and Gabe take seats with me.

"Nah, man, pull up a chair and let's rest a bit. Been a hell of a day," I reply.

Torin nods to me as Chase pulls another chair over. "I wish I had more men like you in my unit back in Iraq, man. It takes a big, steel pair to be the first man into a hole like that, and you were great."

I just snort, then point at the big-ass bruise that still seems to be spreading on my chest. "I wasn't great."

"Yeah, you were," Torin tells me, reaching over to grab my shoulder. "You went in firing, and sent those fucking bastards diving all over the bar. Ain't your fault that boy was a good shot. When you lit up the bar, you knocked his ass down and let us get in. You didn't hesitate, and you helped me...well, you know. Tonight, you helped me start handling my fucking business. You've been a good friend to my brother, to my family. I just want you to know even with everything going on, I appreciate you." Sighing, he looks over and says, "I better go make sure Eddie isn't fucking up War too bad. Get some rest."

Torin gets up and heads back towards the bar. Chase gets up too. "That's why he's a better leader than me, I swear," Chase mumbles, making me crack a grin. "I'm gonna go keep an eye on him 'til he gets settled in for the night, make sure he doesn't get a wild hair up his ass and take off after what he did to Johnny. You take care of yourself. I love you, man. You're as true a brother to me as Torin."

"Bro, save that mushy shit for Sasha," I grumble as Chase gives me a back slapping hug. I push him off of me, and he staggers back laughing before moving to follow Torin.

Gabriel is still sitting at the table, fingering my vest and staring at me. "You almost got yourself killed tonight," he begins, before I raise a hand to silence him.

"Stow that shit, Gabe. You and me, we don't have to bullshit each other. Torin and Chase can give me all their kind words, but you know me, *really* know me. I fucked up tonight, the same as I always do. They don't see it that way, but..."

"Goddammit, Abe. N*obody* sees it that way, except you!" Gabe says in exasperation, interrupting my moping. "I've been trying to pin you down and talk to you about it forever, but you're more hardheaded than old man Turtle! In your head, you've always been a fuck-up, but no one else sees you that way!"

"What the hell is wrong with everyone tonight?" I growl back at him. "Christ, Torin is acting like I'm some sort of hero for going in first. I *had* to go in first. I'm a fucking felon who has spent his entire life letting people down. There's nothing heroic about being a piece of shit and knowing that other people's lives are worth more than yours."

"Abe, if I hear you say that shit ever again, I'm going to..." Gabe begins as he stands up.

"You'll fucking what, you scrawny little son-of-a-bitch?" I roar, standing up to tower over my brother as everyone in the room turns to look at us. As if it wasn't obvious, the two of us had very different fathers. Mine was apparently enormous while his was light and lean.

"I'll wait until you've forgotten about this conversation. And then, when you come to me for your next tattoo, I'll draw the hairiest, most detailed cock and balls the world has ever seen on you," Gabe threatens, whispering so that only I can hear him.

We both burst out laughing before collapsing back into our chairs. "I know you would, too, you dirty bastard," I wheeze as I grab my beer. "You did it to me once before on my hand with a sharpie when we were kids, remember?"

"Seriously, though, Abe," Gabe leans over the table and begins a moment later. "You're not the fuck-up you think you are. You've never let me down, even..."

"Even when my dumbass got arrested and shipped off to juvie, leaving you alone to deal with our momma and whatever crackhead she was banging before you found her foaming out the mouth, OD'ing? I know what they did to you, Gabe. I know what you had to go through. I wasn't there for you."

"That's not fucking on you, Abe. I never blamed you. Jesus, you got arrested that first time for shoplifting food for us. Food, man! You think I don't remember that it was you bringing home boxes of macaroni and cheese and packs of hot dogs most nights for us? You called that shit ghetto alfredo, remember? Momma would be gone for days on benders, and the only reason I survived in that trailer was because of the risks *you* took. You think I don't know who brought the presents from Santa? Shit, you remember Momma would try to steal the art supplies you had gotten for me and go pawn them."

I chuckle softly, remembering those holidays where I had gone out breaking into cars and stealing packages from doorsteps, trying to pawn enough shit to get Gabe the stuff he needed for his drawings. My face hardens, though, knowing all too well how it turned out for him. "Yeah, Gabe, I tried. I tried and I failed. I got locked up and left you alone. What you had to endure..."

"It. Was. Not. Your. Fault." Gabe emphasizes each word with a poke to the bruise on my chest.

I stand up, waving him off as I wince at the pain. "You've said that a thousand times, but the words don't make it true. I hear them, and I appreciate them. I had something happen to me today, before all this," I tell him, waving at the vest and bullet on the table. "Something big, I think. I met someone, and I don't know how it's going to turn out, but...she makes me feel...better. Not about being me, but makes me feel like I could be..."

"You met a girl who makes you want to be a better man?" Gabe says.

"Yeah! You nailed it. That's what I've been trying to find the words to say. I have to see her again. I'm gonna go get cleaned up and get some sleep. Thanks, little man," I tell Gabe, leaning down to squeeze him in a one-armed hug.

"Let me know if I can help, bro," Gabe calls to me as I head downstairs. "And don't do anything too crazy! I don't think you're a fuck-up, but you are...let's call it impulsive?"

I bark out a laugh as I punch in the code and slam the door leading down to the basement, blocking out the sounds from the bar. Despite being shot tonight, I feel good. Damned good actually, and hopeful that maybe, just maybe, I might finally be riding a clear, easy road.

CHAPTER SEVEN

Mercy

THE MORNING AFTER I WAS THOROUGHLY FUCKED BY ONE incredibly big biker, I'm still a little bit sore between my legs as I sit in my Sunday best next to my mother in a church pew. Even with the guilt of being a bad little Christian, it was well worth every second. Never in my life have I done something so spontaneous with a man I just met, knowing it would only be a one-night stand.

Or at least that's what I'm assuming it will be. It's not like Abe asked me for my phone number before he left, so it must not have been good enough for a second round. If it had been, he would've asked Sasha for my number, right? I guess I could always ask her for his to find out...

No, no, no.

This is why women can't have casual sex with strangers. We get attached too easily. And then come all the doubts about ourselves. He hasn't called, so he must prefer prettier women or women with bigger breasts or women who are better...

I have got to start focusing on the upcoming show instead of obsessing about my lapse in judgment. Tomorrow is our photo shoot for promos. Technically, none of the guys are supposed to speak to me so that our first introduction will be with the cameras on us as they pull up in limos, but it'll be nice to at least get to look at them.

Already, I'm guessing that none of them will be as tall as Abe or have his long beard.

Ugh, I need to stop thinking about that man. It's pathetic and makes me seem like a teenage girl obsessing about a boy just because he gave me a few orgasms. Okay, more than half a dozen orgasms, but still. It was a one-time thing that I did because I was ridiculously horny and curious to see if sex with a stranger could be better than with someone you're falling in love with.

So what if I'm a little disappointed that it was a glaringly obvious YES. Who would've known that someone who doesn't know a thing about you other than your name could know their way around your body better than you do?

More stabs of guilt hit me when I'm sitting in church service. Then, those stabs double later that afternoon when I'm meeting with the producers and directors of the *Queen of Hearts*. Even though it was just to get the schedule for the next few weeks, they reminded me that, as part of my contract, I cannot date anyone publicly until after the show finishes airing in around six months. The clock doesn't start ticking until the first day on set, which is two days away; but for whatever reason, I still feel guilty when they are giving me the whole spiel. As long as I don't see Abe again, I won't sleep with him again, so it shouldn't be a problem. He obviously doesn't want to be with me more than the one time, and that's fine. I don't need to dwell on the reasons why.

After I returned home, I did some house cleaning; then changed into a pair of cotton shorts and my sports bra to go for a jog on the warm sandy beach. I don't wear headphones to listen to music while I run, preferring the sounds of the crashing waves and seagulls instead. It's extremely peaceful, and I need to use my time today to stop thinking about a certain biker who had his mouth on a very intimate place on my body. It's probably a good thing that I won't have to see him again after how I came apart for him so easily over and over again. I'm embarrassed that I was so selfish and couldn't be more ladylike, but how does one act ladylike sitting on a man's face? Even though I've never let go like that before or had someone make me feel that good, I'm sure there are plenty of other men who are just as talented. I just haven't met them yet. What if I never do? Oh, god. What if Abe is the best sex of my life and I never have it again with anyone else?

Those are the crazy thoughts that are bouncing around my head when I jog to my front door while unzipping the dorky fanny pack around my waist where I keep my keys and phone while I'm running. I'm so preoccupied that my tennis shoe nearly crushes the single pink rose that's lying on my welcome mat.

A smile stretches across my face before I even realize it's there. Who would've thought that the bearded biker could be so sweet? And does this mean he thought the sex was great too?

I snatch up the rose to bring it to my nose and smell it, and then see that underneath there's also a small, folded piece of white paper with my name handwritten on the front. Wow. A note too? Maybe it says that Abe wants to see me again and he left his phone number. Not that I *can* see him again, but still it's a sweet gesture.

Finally pulling my keys from my pouch, I unlock the front door and head inside to cool off and read the note in the air conditioning. I take a seat on the sofa, placing the rose next to me so that I can break through the staple holding the paper together and read it.

The first neatly typed sentence is confusing. The second sends me for a loop, making me even more confused as I go back and reread the whole entire thing again.

My dearest Mercy,

I can't even begin to tell you how disappointed I am in your incredibly slutty behavior. After waiting a year for you to come back to me, you repay my patience by having intercourse with a man you don't even know rather than me, your undeniable soulmate.

Worst of all, I know that you didn't use a condom because there wasn't a wrapper in the trash you put out today. Don't you know how disgusting that is and how many diseases you could pass on to me by being so careless?

Despite your horrible mistake, I forgive you because I love you, even though you haven't yet realized that I'm the man for you. But you will love me too. I'm sure of that. It's impossible for you to fight the pull toward me forever.

Until that time, don't make the same mistake again.

Your One and Only.

Holy shit.

It's not from Abe.

In fact, I don't know who the hell left such bizarre words.

My first reaction is to the lock the front door, but not even doing that will make me feel safe since whoever the insane person is who wrote the letter could be lurking outside. He must have been here yesterday if he knew I had sex with Abe and then again today when he went through my trash! Yuck. How disgusting.

Without even bothering to change out of my sweaty clothes, I crush the offending paper in my hand. Looking out the window, I check to see if anyone is lurking around. Since I don't see a single soul, I quickly step outside and lock my door before racing toward my car. As soon as the driver's door shuts, I press the button to lock the automatic door and then toss the letter into the passenger seat so that I can crank the engine to hightail it out of my neighborhood.

Since I haven't been back in town for very long or spoken to many people, the first person I think of to call is Sasha, since there's no way I can explain this to my mother. I pull my phone from my fanny pack and carefully call her on speed dial while driving. My hand holding the phone to my ear shakes the whole time it rings.

"Hey, girl!" Sasha answers right away.

"I think I have a stalker," I blurt out since I'm not entirely sure where to begin.

"You have a what? A stalker?" she asks.

"Yes," I reply while checking my rearview to make sure no one is following me when I leave the neighborhood and head north for the highway.

"What happened?" Sasha asks.

"I went for a run and...and when I came back to the house, there was a note with a rose. I thought it was from Abe, you know? But it wasn't. Whoever the hell he is knows what I've been doing and admitted that he went through my trash!"

"Oh, my god," Sasha mutters. "You can't stay there alone!"

"I know!" I reply. "I left. Right now I'm in my car."

"You should come to our place. I'll text you the address. It's off the main roads and so rural that we'll be able to see if someone follows you," she offers.

"Okay, thanks. I'm heading that way now," I say when I take the exit for the northern beaches.

"Be careful!" Sasha warns before we disconnect.

Once she's no longer on the phone, I'm even more terrified because it feels like I'm completely alone. Maybe I should've kept talking to her.

No, that's ridiculous. I'm safe in my car.

Glancing swiftly over my shoulder at the stop sign, I check to make sure there's no one hiding in the backseat like in a scary movie. Nope, all clear, thank goodness.

About half way to the Emerald Isle, I start to wonder if I'm making a big deal out of nothing. Am I overreacting? After I show Sasha the note, I'm sure she'll be honest with me and tell me if I'm freaking out for no reason.

But then, when I get to the main strip of town and I'm sitting at a stoplight, I glance over and see the typed note I tossed in the passenger seat. The words *slutty* and *condom wrapper* jump out, and I'm certain that this is not your garden variety stalker. This person actually went through my things, my trash, for christsakes.

Once I'm in town, it takes me only a few more minutes to follow the directions Sasha sent to my phone.

When I see a truck, a shiny black Harley and her classic Mustang convertible that she's had since she was a teenager in the driveway of a two-story white house, I'm certain I have the right place.

Sasha must have heard me coming. She's running down the porch stairs before I can get out of my car.

I gather up my keys, phone and the note in my hands and then climb out.

"Hey," Sasha says when she meets me in front of the hood of my car and wraps her arms around me.

"Sorry, I'm a mess. I didn't shower after I ran..." I start to say.

"No, don't worry about that. We'll find you some clothes," she says when she pulls away. "So is that the note?" she asks with her eyes lowered to the piece of paper clutched in my hand.

"Yeah," I say. "Read it and see if I'm just being paranoid. Tell me the truth."

Since my hands are a little full, Sasha carefully reaches for the corner of the paper with her two fingertips to pull it free. I watch her face as she reads the words. Her blue eyes widen, and her jaw drops open early on.

When she looks back up at me, she says, "This person is fucking insane!"

I release the breath I didn't know I was holding, relieved that I didn't drive an hour up here for something silly.

"That was my first reaction too," I admit. "But I wasn't sure."

"And we'll have to come back to the part about Abe later," she says with a small smile before she turns toward the house and puts an arm around my shoulders. "Come on in. Do you mind if I show the letter to Chase?"

"No, please do. It'd be nice to get a guy's perspective on it too," I say as I follow her up the steps to the porch. Before I step inside their home, I glance behind me toward the road just to be certain that no one followed me. The gravel road is clear.

"Chase, baby?" Sasha calls out as she starts down a short hallway that leads to the kitchen where her man is washing dishes. If I weren't so freaked out, I'd probably be impressed by how odd a man in a leather cut looks while being all domesticated.

"Yeah, sweetheart?" Chase asks over his shoulder. "Oh, hey, Mercy."

"Hey, sorry for dropping in on such short notice," I tell him.

"You're fine," he says with a shake of his head.

"Read this," Sasha says, holding out the note to him. Chase rinses his hands under the faucet and then dries them off on a dish cloth before taking the piece of paper from her. One of his reddish-blond eyebrows arches within seconds, and then he curses under his breath.

"This dude is certifiable," Chase eventually looks up and tells me and Sasha when he hands the paper back to her and then she gives it to me. I set it down on the counter, because I feel icky just touching something that came from someone so freaking disturbed.

"Mercy should stay here with us tonight, shouldn't she?" Sasha asks Chase when she steps into his side and his arm goes around her back.

"Hell yes," Chase replies. "You shouldn't be alone until you figure out who this fucker is and have him locked up. Any clue who it could be?" he asks.

"No," I answer. "I thought about it on the drive here. And while I've received some pretty intense fan letters through my agent and even some perverted ones, none have actually *known* intimate details like this about me. I mean, I just moved into the house, so how did they know where I lived?" I ask aloud.

"They've been following you," Chase concludes. "Maybe found out where you were thanks to the paparazzi and then were stealthy about following you back home."

"Ugh, I guess so," I say, frowning at the thought of someone watching me without me even realizing it. I feel so...violated.

"I don't know what to do about this," I say on a heavy exhale as I wrap my arms around my waist. "Should I call the police?" I ask them.

"Maybe. But if you don't know who it is, they probably can't do much," Sasha points out.

"That's true," Chase agrees.

"And if I go to the police, it'll probably get out to the media, which will make the paparazzi worse," I add.

"Also, true," Sasha agrees. "But you can't run around on your own. What if this nutcase decides to approach you to prove to you that he's your, what did he call himself again, *your undeniable soulmate?*"

"Righhht," Chase drawls with a roll of his green eyes.

"I have to do something. Tomorrow there's a photo shoot for the show, and then we start filming," I explain in a rush. While what I want most is to hide under the bed until the crazy person gives up, my life has to go on.

Sasha and Chase trade a look with each other; and then both of them grin, making me think that they're plotting something.

"I'm sure Abe wouldn't mind tagging along with you until they catch the weirdo stalker," Chase offers.

"No," I reply automatically with a shake of my head. "That's really not necessary. He probably doesn't want to see me again, and I'm sure he has better things to do..."

"Call him," Sasha tells Chase, completely ignoring my protests. Then, with a kiss on her man's cheek, she pushes away from him and grabs my elbow to lead me out of the kitchen. "I'm sure Abe will be right over. So, until then, how about we find you a shirt while you fill me in on what happened yesterday after you two left the restaurant together?" she says with a smile that tells me there's no way to squirm out of this conversation and also reminds me that I've been wandering around in just my sports bra. Jeez, I'm all messed up.

CHAPTER EIGHT

Abe

IT'S EARLY IN THE AFTERNOON, SO THE BASEMENT LEVEL OF THE clubhouse is pretty empty.

Since no one's in the chapel — Torin, because he's back to his house grieving, and Chase, because he's probably at home with his old lady — I head inside and grab one of the secure laptops sitting on the bookshelf at the back of the room that all of us can use whenever we need. They're handy because none of us carry smartphones. Those bastards are an outlaw's worst enemy. That means, if I need to do some internet research, I have to break out a laptop.

Taking it to my room, I sit down in the chair at the wooden desk and clear a spot in all the random pieces of junk to make room for the computer, then I fire it up.

What am I so intent on searching today?

Birth control.

Crazy, right? I nearly get shot and killed, but all I've been obsessing about is what I did yesterday with Mercy. I mean, it wasn't just the amazing sex, but I'm still freaking out about coming inside of her. And it's not just that I'm worried there's a possibility I knocked her up, it's this strange other emotion that's been trying to bust free from my gut – one that hopes I did. I'm losing my fucking mind, obviously. I busted my first nut while being inside a pussy without a barrier, and now I've lost my shit because of it.

Why didn't anyone tell me how good going bareback is? Is that why people have kids? Because the sex is so mind-blowing that raising a snotty-nosed child for eighteen years is worth the few moments of heaven on Earth? That must be it and would explain why my mother had me and Gabe since she wasn't the maternal type at all.

Anyway, I intend to find out just how effective that birth control shot thing is that Mercy uses to see what the chances are that I've fucked myself over. After everything that happened last night, I know I shouldn't want more of this woman in my life, but I can't let it be because of some fucked-up child situation. My brother and I are all the proof I need that some people shouldn't have kids.

It takes me longer than it should for my thick fingers to peck out the few words in the search engine before the site brings up the answer in the very first article. The shot is apparently more than ninety-nine percent effective at preventing pregnancy when administered correctly.

Whew. Great. Awesome.

That means there's less than a one percent chance that I put a baby in Mercy. So if I fucked her a hundred times, only one of those could make it happen. That's a relief.

I think.

My eyes continue to scan the article, and I see shit like ninety-four percent successful if the shot is *not* administered correctly and possibly less if the woman falls behind on her shot dates.

Oh shit.

When was Mercy's last shot? Does she get them when she's

supposed to? What if she forgot? If she did, there could be a six-percent chance that a mini-Abe is on the way. That's still a small chance, right?

"Someone tired of using condoms?"

I startle and nearly reach for the gun I keep mounted under the desk when dumbass Dalton opens his mouth from right behind me.

"Are you trying to get that pretty boy face of yours blown off?" I ask him before slamming the laptop lid closed.

"Just to warn you, you can still get the clap and all that other shit if she's on the shot," he says, ignoring my threat.

"You would know that from experience, right?" I turn around and ask him.

"Only sharing the facts," he says with a shrug and a smirk. "But I will say that sweet, wet pussy isn't worth the price of the meds."

Shaking my head, I grumble, "What do you want?"

"Checking in on you after you took that bullet yesterday. So, why the research?" he asks, the asshole unable to take a hint.

"None of your business," I mutter as I get to my feet and shove past him to head upstairs. I'm still not one-hundred percent sure that Dalton isn't the rat in our club. He kicked ass at that Aces' bar last night right alongside the rest of us. Was that all just an act? I hate doubting one of my brothers, but Chase is certain that someone was reporting shit back to Hector Cruz, and his reasoning makes sense. Guess only time will tell who is loyal and who is not.

With that asshat reminding me of STDs, I figure I better go and get tested. Not because I'm worried that Mercy gave me something, but to make sure she's protected from me. I've always used condoms in the past, but what if something slipped through the cracks? Mercy trusted me, so I want to make sure that I'm safe for her.

Sure, it's painful to have the swab shoved up your dick hole, but it's worth it for me to know in a few days that I'm free and clear. It's been a year since my last checkup, so better safe than sorry.

I've just stepped out of the clinic a couple of hours later when my phone rings. Only my brothers have this burner phone's number, so I know it's important. Seeing that it's Chase calling, I don't let it ring again before I answer.

"What's up, brother?" I ask.

"Can you come over to the house?" he asks, and I can tell by the tone of his voice that's he's annoyed.

"Sure. Everything okay?"

"Yeah, Mercy's here," he says, and my entire body lights up like it's Christmas at the thought of seeing her again, especially my cock.

Was it just yesterday that I ate her out for an hour and then she rode me on her living room floor? Hell, I guess it was, but it seems like longer.

Chase doesn't need to tell me anything else. I end the call, strap on my helmet, and take off down the road on my bike, planning to get to Chase and Sasha's place in record-breaking time.

...

Mercy

"So you and Abe did the nasty?" Sasha turns to me and asks with a grin after she drags me upstairs to the bedroom I assume she shares with Chase, then shuts the door.

Sighing, because there's no way I can deny that I slept with him after she read the stalker letter, and certain that Sasha is bringing it up most likely because she's trying to take my mind off of the whole ordeal, I say, "Yes."

"Yay!" she cheers before sitting on their neatly made bed and patting the spot next to her. "Sit. Give me all of the details."

Okay, so she's also a little nosy too, but I love her like the sister I never had but always wanted, so I sit down and start to spill. Or try to. It's harder than I thought to admit aloud that I had sex with a man I just met. Covering my face with my hands, I say, "I don't know what the heck I was thinking."

"You were thinking that he was a big, hot biker who looked like an expert in knowing the best ways to make a woman scream," Sasha supplies, making my hands drop from my face and my jaw drop so that I can face her.

"Sasha!" I chastise.

"Am I wrong?" she asks with a smirk.

"No, but still..."

"I only know because I've been there too," she points out, implying a little more than I needed to know about her and Chase. "So, were you right about him?" she asks.

Taking a deep breath to consider my words, I finally admit to her, "I nearly lost my voice."

"I knew it!" Sasha exclaims triumphantly with both of her arms in the air. "Start from the beginning. What happened after you left the restaurant?"

"We just went for a ride, stopped and talked for a while. Flirted a little," I answer with a shrug.

"And then?"

"And then he took me home..." I start before I narrow my eyes at her. "You wouldn't know anything about that dime in the seat of my car, would you?"

"What? No way," she answers with an indignant scoff. "I'm sure it just fell out of my pocket."

"You were wearing a dress without pockets," I point out.

"Oh, then it fell out of my purse," she replies with a mischievous grin.

"I take it you're familiar with Abe's 'Beard rides' shirt?"

Tapping her fingernail to her lip as if she's thinking about it,

Sasha eventually says, "You know, I may be familiar with such a shirt."

"Of course you are," I mutter with a shake of my head. "And I'm sure I wasn't the first woman to saddle up."

"Abe isn't a womanizer," Sasha contends, making me roll my eyes. "He isn't! Yes, there are a few women at the clubhouse that he gets...*consoled* by, but they love him."

"Wow. That makes me feel better," I reply sarcastically.

"No, I mean, those women may be a little clingy, but believe me, they know the score. The guys don't lead them on, yet they keep coming back for more."

"Well, I won't be going back for more," I assure her. "And he obviously isn't interested in more either."

"You won't? He's not?" she asks, arching one of her blonde eyebrows skeptically.

"No. It was a one-time thing. Besides, even if I wanted...more good times, I have the show coming up."

"We both know that you're not going to be able to open up and find the man of your dreams on a reality show," Sasha declares. "Especially not after what happened with..."

"Yes, I know that whole thing with Blake messed with my head and heart, but the producers swear that they found the twenty men for the show based on various personality tests that match exactly what I said I'm looking for in a husband."

"I'm sure they did find some suitable matches for you," Sasha says. "But they're also looking for ratings, which means there will be some men who are super competitive, some that are funny, and some that are complete assholes when they're on camera but sweethearts when they're with you. Like Blake."

"Probably," I admit. "And if I don't like a single one of them, then I'll act like I do until the finale for great ratings."

"Pretend and possibly break someone's heart like Blake did to you?" Sasha asks.

"No. I'm not going to lead anyone on, and I am definitely not sleeping with any of them," I assure her. "If the producers want to make it look like we shut the door and more happened for the sake of the curious viewers, then fine. But I'm not tangling up the physical stuff with the emotional."

"Did any of the emotional get tangled up with the physical stuff you did with Abe?" Sasha asks with a grin.

"No, of course not," I reply with a scoff. "I barely know him, and it was more of an experiment."

"An experiment?" Sasha repeats with her brow furrowed.

"Yeah, an experiment to see if sex with a stranger can be as good as it is with someone you have feelings for."

"And what's the verdict?" she asks. "I've never slept with a stranger."

"Maybe Abe was an anomaly," I say while I examine my fingernails. "But I don't think I could ever have sex with anyone who will top that."

"Aww," Sasha says as if what I said was meant to be sweet.

"It was just sex."

"Great sex?" she amends.

"Yes."

"Amazing sex?"

"That too," I answer. "Honestly, there's not an adjective in the dictionary that would accurately describe how good it was, at least for me. Now I know why so many women fall for bad boys."

"Because they do it better," Sasha agrees seriously with a nod of her head.

Thinking back to the hazy memories of the day before, I admit, "No one's ever treated me like...that."

"Like what?" Sasha asks. "Like you're a dirty little slut who's been bad and needs to be punished?"

"Um, not quite," I say as I blink at her in surprise from another bout of TMI. Clearing those thoughts from my head, I think back to last night and say, "Abe looked at me and...and touched me like his sole purpose in this world was to make me feel good."

"So you would say that, in a way, he sort of worshipped you?" Sasha asks as she gets to her feet and chews on her bottom lip.

"No, that's not what I meant," I correct her.

"Adored you?" she throws out.

"I-I dunno. Maybe, yeah?" I reply like I'm asking her for the answer. "It was sort of one-sided. I mean, maybe I was being selfish..."

"Have you thought about him all day?" Sasha questions me.

"Well, sure. I mean, how could I not after what we did together?" I say.

"You're smiling," she points out.

"So?" I ask in confusion.

"Do you want to be with him again?"

"I can't," I remind her. "The show and all..."

"But you would want to be with him if not for the show and shit?" she asks.

God, yes.

I'm surprised when my head answers so adamantly before my mouth can even open.

"I wouldn't be opposed to such a notion," I tell her with a casual shrug of my shoulders.

"Oh, my god!" Sasha exclaims. "You're falling for him!"

"What? No way!" I reply. "How could I fall for him when I don't even know him? Heck, I don't even know his last name! It was just great sex. Once. Now it's over. Besides, he doesn't want more or he would've asked for my number!"

"You've never slept with a man you've just met before, have you?" she points out. "So why Abe?"

Throwing my hands up in the air, I say, "I told you, I don't know what I was thinking. Obviously, I wasn't. And it could've been a huge disaster. Maybe I thought he was safe since I figured you wouldn't have trusted him to take me home if you didn't approve. I also thought it could be my last chance at a casual romp with no strings attached before I find Mr. Right."

Sasha is grinning like a lunatic. "I wasn't sure what you would think about Abe. I mean, he's not your usual type, but those arrogant assholes you dated weren't working. But I knew without a doubt you were his type."

"I'm his type?" I blurt out in surprise while warmth fills my chest and some of the gaping holes caused by self-doubt. "I didn't think men like him had a type."

"Abe *loves* redheads," she informs me, which makes a lot of sense when I think back to his comments about me being a natural redhead...

"There it is again!" Sasha shouts so loudly that I startle.

"What?" I ask.

"That smile on your face that makes me think I am an awesome matchmaker," she replies with a smug grin, even doing a goofy little cabbage patch meets running man dance that has me snorting.

"Do you have any idea how ridiculous you look?" I ask her.

"Laugh all you want," Sasha tells me. "But you are on your way to becoming an old lady."

My jaw falls open before I say, "Rude! I'm the same age as you!"

"No, silly," she tells me with a laugh. "That's what the guys in the MC call their women."

"Oh," I mutter as I cross my arms over my chest and realize I'm still wearing just a sports bra. "Well, it's still rude," I point out.

"You'll get used to it," she tells me with a wave of her hand. "Now, let's find you a shirt to wear and then get back downstairs to wait for your man."

"My man?" I repeat. "You've lost your mind. It was a one-time thing that won't ever happen again! He doesn't want more, and I can't do it again."

"It only takes one time to start a full-fledged love affair," she tells me. "And who knows what will happen with him playing the role of your bodyguard."

"Ugh, and just when I was starting to forget the stalker," I tell her.

"Abe will keep you safe from that maniac," Sasha assures me before she turns toward her closet, muttering something that sounds like, "Even if he has to kill him."

CHAPTER NINE

Abe

I'm a little thrown when I walk up Chase and Sasha's porch and find that the door is still closed and locked up tight even though they're expecting me. Raising my knuckles, I rap swiftly on the door, in a hurry to see the redheaded goddess again. Also, we need to have another talk about her birth control.

Chase finally opens the door after what feels like an hour later.

"Hey, man," I say when he lets me in and then immediately shuts and locks the door again. "Something up?" I ask since his shoulders are tense, and his eyes keep looking out the window.

"Come on in and see for yourself," he grumbles.

I follow him to the kitchen where Sasha and Mercy are sitting at the dining table that's full of food, bowls of pasta and vegetables, both women looking like someone pissed in their plates. Mercy's emerald eyes lower from mine way too soon, though, before I can try to read them.

"You got here fast," Sasha teases. She barely breaks a smile, trying to refrain from making fun of me rushing over to see Mercy. I

89

glance over at the redhead again and notice she's wearing a baggy, white t-shirt that looks like she stole it from some dude. I don't like that at all.

"Here," Chase says and then thrusts a piece of paper in front of my face.

I flip it over and see it has typed print on one side and just Mercy's name handwritten on the other. What kind of shit is this? Why is he giving me a note that someone sent her? Does he want me to be jealous? If so, mission accomplished.

Then I actually start reading. I feel my face warming with anger a little more with each word. Who the fuck would dare call this classy woman slutty? And did they seriously go digging through her garbage looking for a used rubber? That's sick fucking shit.

"Who the fuck wrote this?" I roar as I hold the offending paper up in the air and look to Mercy for a name. As soon as I get one, I'll kick his fucking ass.

"I don't know," she replies softly, looking so timid with her arms wrapped around herself that I finally notice how scared she is. That's why she came here to Chase and Sasha's place, because some psycho freak has been creeping around her house. Wow. What if he had tried to break in and hurt her?

Lowering my voice along with my anger, I tell her, "I'm sorry."

"We thought you might want to hang out with Mercy until this fucker is caught," Chase informs me.

"You don't have to–" Mercy starts before I interrupt her.

"Abso-fucking-lutely," I agree. If anyone tries to hurt her on my watch, I'll blow his goddamn head off. Who the hell does he think he is? Her *soulmate*? Really? That's the biggest load of horse shit I've ever read.

"You're both welcome to stay here tonight, if you want," Sasha offers.

I lift an eyebrow to Chase since I won't crash in his home unless he says it's okay.

"Yeah, man. I bet Reece can get his hands on some high-tech

security equipment. You two probably don't want to stay at Mercy's until it's installed," Chase says, barely hiding his smile. I bet he'll give me hell about how I'm already twisted up about his old lady's friend. And he'll be right. If he called me a bowl full of pussy whip with a cherry on top, I wouldn't even deny it.

"Fine," I agree even though we would be safe at her place if I were there with her. Unless I got distracted and shit when we started fucking again.

Oh, fuck.

As long as this asshole stalker is out there watching her, I won't lay a hand on Mercy. I can't afford to be distracted, because there's no telling what crazy shit the fucker may try to do to her. So, no matter how much I'm dying to touch her or taste her again, I won't screw this up. Her safety is more important than me getting off.

"You had dinner yet, Abe?" Sasha asks.

"No."

"Then sit down and dig in. We have plenty," she tells me. "Here, you can take my seat. I'm finished," Sasha says when she stands up from the chair that's closest to Mercy to take her plate over to the sink. "Chase and I will go get everything ready in the spare bedroom," she adds before she grabs the front of Chase's cut and pulls him along behind her so that Mercy and I are alone.

If I had to guess, I think Sasha has some absurd notion that Mercy and I could be a couple if she keeps pushing the two of us together. And while that would be a nice dream, it's never going to be the reality. The two of us are complete opposites living worlds apart.

Taking Sasha's vacant seat, I grab a bowl full of some sort of pasta in white sauce and pull it to me to dig in with the big serving fork that's still in it.

"Hey," I say to Mercy after I chew the first bite. I hate the awkward silence between us.

"Hey," she replies.

Cramming in another mouthful, I chew and swallow, then ask, "How often do you get your shot?"

"Excuse me?" she asks with a cute little wrinkle forming between her red brows.

"Your birth control shot," I elaborate.

"Oh," she mutters in understanding. "Um, every three months."

"You get them on time?"

"Yes," she replies slowly. "Why?"

"Just making sure I didn't knock you up," I grumble softly.

"Don't worry. I always get the shot when I'm supposed to. It's not like I want kids either. Well, not yet," she says as her fingers begin to fidget with her napkin. "Other than reassurances about my birth control, did you have any other questions or, you know, comments about yesterday?" she asks.

"Nope," I reply since I think she's being sarcastic and I'm still hung up on the kid thing.

Of course she wants kids and I don't. Ever. Just another reason why the two of us would never be able to have more than a few incredible orgasms together. An actual relationship would never work between us. Not that I'm capable of a relationship with any woman...

But the fact that Mercy wants kids means that someday in the future she'll want a man to put kids in her belly. And now I'm suddenly jealous of this future, hypothetical asshole who gets to touch her because I can't. Fuck, do I want to, though.

As if she's sensing those thoughts, Mercy says, "What we did...it was great, at least for me, but it can't happen again."

"I fucking know that," I grumble, because I figured that out a few seconds earlier or maybe even yesterday when she kicked me out. And I really like hearing her say that sex with me was great even though I was well aware of that too. I think I'm a pretty damn good lover all of the time, but I've never enjoyed fucking as much as I did with Mercy.

"And you don't have to follow me around..." she starts.

"Yes, I do," I interrupt before I continue eating.

"No, you don't, Abe," she argues. "I could go to the police or –"

"Fuck the police," I huff. I put the bowl of pasta down and lick my lips to clean them. "I can protect you better than they can."

"Oh, so you can do it better than all of them? The entire Wilmington Police Department?" Mercy asks with the corners of her lips raised.

"Yes," I answer flatly. I would take on anyone for Mercy, even an army of scrawny little cops.

"It's probably nothing," she says.

"That note is a helluva lot more than nothing," I tell her. "He sounds unreasonably possessive and seriously angry at you for no damn reason. Do you really want to wait and see if he's possessive and angry enough to actually hurt you?"

"Well, no," Mercy answers with her shoulders hunched in the baggy, white shirt.

"Damn right you don't. If he comes back, I'll take care of him," I tell her. "Our brother, Reece, can install a high-tech security camera in your house too."

"He doesn't have to–" she starts.

"Yes, he does," I declare with a slap of my palm on the table to try and cut off her arguing.

"I don't remember you being this bossy yesterday," Mercy says.

"Oh really?" I ask as I slouch back in the chair to give my aching cock a little more room to grow in my jeans. "Because I remember you nearly breaking an ankle to get inside your house and get naked for me."

...

Mercy

AND THERE IT IS.

Just when I thought that I could be in the same room as Abe without any shame or embarrassment about what we did together yesterday, he has to go and say things that...things that make my lower belly warm and tighten like it's a volcano that's ready to erupt. Which isn't far from the truth. All it took was a few gruff words from him and my panties turn into the physical proof that it wouldn't take much more than a touch of one of Abe's thick fingers, talented tongue or huge cock to cause an explosion.

"Fine, so yes, I had a momentary lapse forgetting your bossiness," I tell him. "But could we please not bring all that up in our normal conversation since it's not going to happen again?" I really don't need to hear another man complain about how selfish or frigid I am.

"Right," Abe says.

"And I'm pretty tired, so I think I'll head upstairs to get a shower and go to bed," I declare as I push my chair back and get to my feet. Mostly because I need to relieve the building pressure between my legs or I may have a spontaneous orgasm from just being in the same room as Abe.

"Right," Abe says again. "I'll, ah, call Reece and see how long it'll take to get a security system installed."

"Thanks," I tell him rather than try to talk him out of playing the part of my bodyguard or telling him a security system is unnecessary. The truth is, I already feel much safer knowing Abe will be close by, and the added precautions won't hurt.

Now, if I could just figure out who the hell left me the rose and the note.

Heading up the stairs, I find Sasha and Chase in one of the other bedrooms, putting linens on the bed.

"Your room is ready," Sasha tells me as she smooths out the wrinkles in the comforter and then straightens.

"Thank you, both of you, for letting me stay. The thought of going back to my house tonight just makes me feel really creepy," I say, barely able to contain a full body shiver.

"Anytime," Sasha says when she comes over and gives me another hug. "The bathroom in the hallway is all yours since Chase and I use the one in his parents' old room."

"Great. I'll probably take a quick shower before calling it a night," I tell her.

"We're right across the hall if you need anything," Sasha says before she leaves.

I follow them out, eager to rinse off the sweat and try to cool my hormones under the shower spray.

In the bathroom, I close and lock the door, and then start the water running while I undress, deciding instead to soak in a warm bath rather than stand. When the water is high enough, I step over into the tub and lower myself into the sloshy depths.

Instantly, all the coiled muscles in my arms, legs, back and neck begin to relax. I rest my head on the shower wall and try to soak up the peacefulness.

"How long will it take? No, man that's too long. You need to get it here faster! I don't care how much it costs."

Abe's gruff, angry voice filters up the bathroom window from outside where he must be talking on his phone since I can only hear his side of the conversation.

He sounds so bossy and demanding, which only makes the throbbing between my legs even worse. Just hearing him speak shouldn't turn me on as much as it does.

Needing some relief, I ease my hand down my stomach and underneath the water until my fingertips are pressed against my clitoris. I close my eyes and try to remember the way it felt to have Abe's tongue in the same spot yesterday while I touch myself, but nothing happens. I don't know if it's because I'm in my best friend's house trying to masturbate in her tub, but I can't recapture the feeling on my own. How absurd am I right now?

Eventually, after the water turns cool, Abe's voice disappears, and there's still no relief in sight, I give up on the attempt to relieve some stress. After pulling the drain stopper, I stand up and grab the towel on the closest rack to dry off.

Since my sports bra and panties were so sweaty from my run, I decide to forgo them and simply put the t-shirt Sasha let me borrow back on and then slip on my athletic shorts. With my underwear in my hands, I step out of the bathroom and come face to face with a bearded giant. Even though both men in the house were wearing the same leather cut and jeans, I don't even have to look up to know the one in front of me is Abe. He's taller and probably twice as wide as Chase.

"Hey," he says. "Are those your panties?"

"Um, yes," I reply before I hide the clothing behind my back and look up to see his face. Those dark, intense eyes are focused on my chest that's still a little damp and practically see-through in the white cotton. As if aware of his gaze, my nipples harden into points like they're loving Abe's undivided attention.

While I would love to just slip into the bedroom and end the awkward standoff, it's impossible to get past Abe unless I want to get down on all fours and crawl through his legs.

Which would put me...right at eyelevel with his boastful bulge growing behind his zipper.

Great, I'm standing in my best friend's hallway, scantily dressed, staring at a man's crotch while he stares at my breasts.

"I was just, um, going to my room," I tell Abe, hoping he'll get the hint and move.

"Oh. Right," he replies. I glance up at his face and find that his eyes are still focused on my nipples. "I just wanted to let you know that I talked to Reece, our IT genius. He said he'll have a security system here and installed by tomorrow night."

"Oh, thanks," I reply, assuming that's what he was fussing about on the phone earlier. Earlier, when I was trying to masturbate while thinking about him. "Let me know how much I owe you..." I start before Abe interrupts, as is becoming his habit.

"I can pay for it. I'm not as poor as I look," he snaps.

"I-I didn't think you were...poor," I tell him.

"Whatever. I'll cover the costs," he says before he finally turns to the side so that I can get past him.

"Okay. Well, goodnight," I say.

"Night," he replies. Then, he turns and goes back down the stairs before I can even blurt out a pitiful invitation for him to join me in the bedroom to give me the relief I couldn't find on my own.

CHAPTER TEN

Abe

THE NEXT MORNING I'M TIRED AND GRUMPY AS FUCK FROM NOT getting any sleep. How could I when the sexiest woman in the world was sleeping right up the stairs. After seeing her in the hallway without a bra on, I wanted to be in that room with her. No, not just with her but inside of her.

But Mercy didn't give me any indication that I was welcome in her bed, and my job was to watch out for her, so I crashed on the sofa instead of Chase and Sasha's other guestroom. That would've put me in a bed too close to Mercy. Besides, I wanted to keep an eye on the driveway to make sure the creep, who is apparently obsessed with her, didn't follow her to the farmhouse.

As soon as Mercy woke up and came downstairs, she said she had to go home to get ready. I followed her back to her place on my bike so that she could shower and whatever else women do.

While she's in her bathroom, I wander through the entire one-story house and make sure that all of the locks on the windows are in

LANE HART & D.B. WEST

place, then pull all the blinds closed so no one can look in on Mercy when she's undressing or just going about her daily routine.

I didn't realize how exhausted I really was until Mercy steps into the living room. She's wearing a purple dress that crisscrosses at her waist and hugs her curves. Just the sight of her nearly knocks me off my feet.

"I'm ready," she says before I can tell her how hot she looks. "I love the bike, but I guess we better take my car today?"

"Yeah," I agree, my voice so husky that it sounds more like "eh." And she loves my bike? I can't wait to have her on the back of it again.

After I check the yard to make sure it's clear and then lock up the house tight, I go around and squeeze into the passenger seat of her BMW. Once I'm seated, I have to quickly find the lever to move the seat backward because my knees are digging into the damn dashboard.

Mercy's giggle in the silence has my heavy eyes cutting to hers. I throw her a gruff, "What?" even though the sound of her laughing is beautiful just like her, and it makes me want to pull her onto my lap and kiss her pouty, red lips. I didn't even kiss her on the lips the other day, did I? I'm such a moron.

"You're too big for my car," Mercy says, smiling her perfect smile that's contagious.

"I'm not too big," I tell her while adjusting the seat as far as it will go and then resting my palms on my thighs. "See, I fit."

"Barely," Mercy points out as she looks up to where my hair is grazing the roof. "Will the seatbelt go around you?"

"Yes," I huff. "I'm not a fat ass."

"I wasn't implying that you were," she responds. "You're a big man, that's all. There's nothing wrong with that. You look...capable."

"Capable?" I repeat.

"Yeah," she says. "Capable of picking men up by their necks and throwing them around like the Hulk."

"The angry, green man?"

"Yeah, but a lot of women like that. They want a protector who they can depend on to keep them safe," she tells me as she buckles her seatbelt.

And yeah, my chest puffs out a little at the thought of her seeing me as her protector. That's why I'm hanging out with her today, right? To keep any psychos away. Whatever the reason, I like being hers, even if the only reason she wants me around is to protect her. That must be it since she didn't invite me into her bedroom last night. Mercy said the sex was great but not great enough to fuck me again.

Which blows.

It would've sucked to have to be near her if I didn't know how sweet her pussy tasted or how incredible it feels to be inside of her without a rubber. But now that I do know all of those things, it's going to be fucking torture to stop myself from getting distracted when I'm supposed to be acting as her bodyguard.

We get parked in front of the huge warehouse type building, and then I walk Mercy straight inside to a room that actually has her name on the door. It's a little impressive, and I want to take a photo of it when she's not looking.

I take it that this is supposed to be Mercy's dressing room since it's full of racks of clothes and bright ass lights around mirrors. Two random women come in a moment later, moving in a hurry as one starts rubbing shit on Mercy's face and the other takes a hot iron thing to her hair. Why are they doing all that? I have no fucking clue since her face and hair looked gorgeous the way she had it after her shower. Hell, the woman even looked amazing right out of bed this morning when she came down the stairs.

"So, ah, what's this show about?" I ask Mercy as the two women continue to frantically work on her and she sits stock-still like a statue of a Greek goddess.

"It's a, ah, a dating show," Mercy answers.

"A fucking *dating* show?" I repeat.

"Uh-huh."

"So you signed up to date some random guy on television?" I ask, unable to wrap my head around the idea.

"Something like that..."

"There are actually twenty guys," the hairdresser person, who is obviously eavesdropping on our conversation, casually throws out.

"Twenty!" I exclaim, and without moving her head, Mercy's green eyes cut to mine and narrow as if to warn me to cool it.

"My bodyguard is concerned about my safety around so many *strangers*," Mercy tells the hairdresser. And I get that she put an emphasis on strangers since she and I have only known each other for two days. I don't care for the way she refers to me as just her bodyguard either, even if that is the only title I have. For whatever reason, I want to make a t-shirt that proclaims that I've had my tongue in Mercy's pussy for so long I can still taste her even days after the act. And I swear I can. Even if it was just one time, it seems important enough to broadcast my accomplishment. I doubt Mercy feels the same, however.

"So why do you need to be on a dating show? I'm guessing you don't have any problems getting asked out," I mutter.

"It's a big draw from viewers," she replies. "They love the drama of eliminating women, or in my case, men, until I pick 'the one.'"

"The one?" I repeat with a scoff. Does she mean like the man of her dreams or some bullshit? "You think you'll find that in a group of random asshats?"

"Maybe," she answers with a smile. "I fell for Blake that way, so it happens."

"Blake?" The sound of his name tastes as nasty and bitter as spraying lemon juice directly on my tongue.

"He was the *King of Hearts* last season, and I was one of twenty women," she explains.

"Could he be the loser who wrote the note?" I ask.

Again, I get that angry, narrowed-eyed look from her that's a silent demand that I shut up. It's also sexy as fuck to see her beautiful face try to look all angry. She fails and looks adorable instead.

Adorable? Fuck, I've turned into a full-blown pussy.

"It wasn't from him," Mercy snaps in his defense.

"How do you know?"

"Because he picked someone else. Now they're married, living happily ever after in Bali," she answers with a tone of voice that implies she doesn't approve of that shit. "At least that's what I've heard."

It hits me that from the tension in her voice and defensiveness that this son of a bitch hurt her.

How could he pick *any* woman over Mercy? She's fucking perfect. Not just in the looks department either, but god, she's sexy and sweet and there's no one who could compare to her. Does she actually miss the fucker?

And while she may believe that the asshole is living a happy life with someone else, I think I'll still find out his last name and have Reece do a search on him to make sure he isn't hanging around in town. To me, the bastard seems like the most likely suspect – the dumb ass who passed up an opportunity to be with Mercy. Then, when his stupidity eventually caught up to him, he realized how badly he fucked up and is trying to fix it.

Mystery solved. Mercy's stalker *has* to be her fucking ex.

...

"IT'S NOT HER EX," Reece says to me on the phone a few minutes later when I call him. He's easily able to figure out the dickhead's full name with a few clicks on a keyboard and the name of the show.

"How can you be sure?" I ask.

"Because Blake Burton hasn't left Bali. In fact, according to his credit card history, this morning he bought groceries. Now I'm looking at him sitting on his deck through his doorbell camera."

"Fuck," I mutter. If he's crossed off the list of suspects, then we're back to square one. "You got the security system in yet?" I ask Reece, since he ordered it last night and had it overnighted despite the fact that the shipping fees are as much as the system itself. I don't care what it costs. I told him I'd pay him back, because Mercy needs to have her house monitored ASAP.

"Jesus, man. Not yet. I told you I would bring it over and install it as soon as it gets in."

"Fine," I grumble.

"You just need to focus on watching your girl's back for now," Reece tells me. I don't bother correcting his comment that she's my girl. "That note you texted me a copy of last night is obviously from someone with a very serious, very dangerous obsession with her. Those types of people can't be reasoned with. Their reality doesn't exist the same as ours. And if pushed, he could become extremely volatile. You staying so close to her could easily be what sets him off."

"He can bring that shit right to me," I declare. "The sooner the better to get him put away and out of Mercy's life."

"Looking through FBI profiles, if I had to guess, he's probably socially withdrawn and rather timid in person. Likely unremarkable features. In other words, your average Joe who spends way too much time isolating himself from the real world."

"Hmm," I grunt. That could be any damn body. "That sounds sort of like you," I tease him.

"Fuck you. I'm not average looking or isolated, despite my many attempts. Instead, I have to deal with one of you fuckers bothering me every damn day," Reece responds grumpily, making me grin.

When Mercy steps out of her dressing room with bouncy, red curls draped over her fair shoulders, wearing a short and sexy, white dress showing way too much cleavage, I tell Reece, "Gotta go," then abruptly end the call.

Jesus. No wonder this woman has a stalker. I'm on the verge of becoming a certifiable one myself. But I'm not just perving on her from afar. The way I'm looking at her leaves no doubts for Mercy about how much I want her again, even though I can't have her.

"Aren't you going a little too far?" I ask her.

"What?" Mercy asks with her red brows furrowing.

"How do you expect any man to look at you wearing *that* without throwing wood?"

Mercy lets out a small burst of laughter before she shakes her head. "You say whatever pops into your head, don't you?"

"Yeah," I reply. "What's wrong with that?" I ask.

"Nothing," she answers. "I like your honesty. It makes me think that the things you say are actually true."

"Of course they are. Why would I make shit up?" I ask in confusion.

Exhaling heavily, she says, "You'd be surprised how many people hide those real thoughts and just tell people what they *think* they want to hear."

"Well, I'd be shit out of luck if I only said what I thought people wanted to hear. I'm fucking clueless most of the time."

"You're not clueless; you're just authentic," Mercy tells me. "It's nice," she adds with another stunning smile before she struts away, her white high heels clacking on the concrete floor and her ass swaying hypnotically underneath her tight dress. I can't help but wonder what kind of panties she has on. A white thong maybe? Damn, I want to find out, but I need to spend less time worrying about her panties and more time looking around for dudes who look at Mercy like they literally worship the ground her long, gorgeous legs walk on.

This job may be harder than I expected.

...

THAT TORTURE of mine I was so worried about is proven absolutely fucking true a few minutes later when I have to watch twenty fucking assholes drooling over Mercy. While some dick with a clipboard told the men not to speak to Mercy and just pose for their photos, there wasn't any need for words. All of their greedy eyes said the same things – they wanted to fuck my woman.

Well, just because I fucked her once doesn't mean she's *mine*, but I did have her before any of them. And I guarantee that none of them could make her body shake as many times as I did.

Fuck.

I have to stop thinking about that shit. My cock is starting to swell, and I think being a "bodyguard" with a hard-on for the woman I'm supposed to be looking out for is generally frowned upon.

Since none of the men touch Mercy unless specifically directed to by the photographer, all I can do is cross my arms over my chest and glare at them, trying to decide if any look like the type to dig through trash looking for rubbers that have been inside of Mercy.

Several dickheads take notice of me and go rigid with fear. They should be afraid of me. I'd snap their necks if they even *think* the wrong things about Mercy.

The prissy photographer throws me an exasperated look over his shoulder before he walks up to Mercy and says something to her that causes her eyes to jump over to mine. Giving the photographer a nod and a smile, Mercy strolls on over to me, which means that no less than twenty sets of eyes watch her ass leave. More if you count the production crew that's also hanging around holding lights and reflective shit.

"What's up?" I ask without uncrossing my arms when Mercy's standing right in front of me.

"The photographer asked if you could please wait for me outside the room."

"What?" I snap. "Why the fuck would I do that?"

"Apparently you're making the guys a little stiff and uncomfortable," she explains.

"I'm just standing here," I say, holding my arms out to the side.

"Exactly," Mercy replies with a small smile. "You're intimidating."

"Isn't that what bodyguards are supposed to do?" I ask. "Intimidate jackasses?"

"Yes, but I'm safe in here."

"How do you know that for certain?" I point out with an arched eyebrow.

"Because I just met these guys," she says while gesturing with her thumb over her shoulder. "Most, if not all, probably just got into town very recently, so the letter probably couldn't have come from any of them."

"Everyone is a suspect," I tell her. "Except for your ex."

Mercy's eyes widen at the mention of the asshole. "I told you it wasn't Blake."

"Well, I wanted to make sure," I reply. "Reece did a check on him. He's in the clear."

"Good. Great," Mercy says with a nod, but crosses her arms over her chest now as if she's pissed off for some reason. "Anyway, will you wait for me in the hallway or in my dressing room? We shouldn't be much longer."

"I don't like leaving you," I tell her, sighing heavily with my hands braced on my hips.

"It's fine. You'll be right down the hall, so close that you'll hear me if I scream."

A smirk stretches across my face at the reminder. "Yeah, I'm pretty familiar with the sound of your screams."

Smiling even while her eyes lower from mine like she's a little embarrassed by my comment, Mercy shakes her head and slaps a hand against my chest playfully. "Go," she says. Then, she turns around and swishes her ass right back in front of the camera. Before I leave, I give every last dick in the room an angry glare in warning.

CHAPTER ELEVEN

Mercy

AS SOON AS THE HEAVY DOOR SLAMS SHUT BEHIND ABE'S enormous frame, an unusual nervous tingle causes the hair on the back of my neck to stand up.

I know I'm being ridiculous, but what if Abe was right and one of the people in this room is my psycho stalker? No, that's impossible. These men don't even know me...

"Smile, Mercy," Cyrus, the show's photographer directs me when I don't realize that my fake smile slipped.

I paste the smile back on my face and turn this way and that at his direction while sneaking glimpses of the guys around me. While they're all indisputably handsome, none of them really spark my interest. They seem so...small. I'm guessing most are around six feet tall; but after being around a giant the last few days, none of them look like they add up to him. And I'm not just thinking about height either.

The vibe I get from most of these guys without them speaking a word is that they're...pretentious and arrogant, sort of like how Blake was. And while confidence in a man is sexy, too much can make them think they're god's gift to women. Those would be the cheaters, as my mom would point out.

What vibe do I get around Abe? Well, every time he sees me, his eyes go so dark that he looks like he's seconds away from tearing off my clothes and slamming me against the nearest hard surface.

Not that I mind.

And I know exactly how damn good he is at what happens after clothes are removed from the equation. Except...I didn't get to see him without his clothes on. Which is pretty disappointing. Our first time was pretty much all about me.

First time?

I say that like there will be a second time when there can't be, especially since Abe hasn't actually said he wants to be with me again or tried to touch me. I could be completely wrong about the way he looks at me, seeing something that's not really there.

Besides, as soon as the show starts filming tomorrow night, I'm not allowed to date anyone. At least not publicly, since a photo of me with a man who is not on the show being published in a tabloid would kill the illusion of the show — that I'm here to find love. And I *am* going to try to find love, as well as abide by that contract. I need the money to pay not just my bills, but my mother's as well. When my mom and I went to Europe like she's always dreamed of, I splurged maybe a little too much, so my savings is quickly becoming depleted. It seemed like a necessary expense at the time to allow me to keep moving so that I wouldn't have time to think about a certain heartbreaker.

Surprisingly enough, being back here on the photoshoot set where I first saw Blake isn't bringing up as many memories as I thought it would. Guess I have my stalker to thank for that, since my thoughts have been centered around whoever has been watching me and going through my trash. My safety right now takes precedence over falling for a man, believing everything he told me was true, and then getting crushed when I realized how wrong about him I truly was. I'm starting to think that what Blake did hurt me even more because he turned things around to make himself look better. He was leading me on, but turned the tables on me by saying he suddenly realized I was fake and bad in bed when he was just covering his ass for sleeping with two women without them knowing about it for weeks!

Well, screw that man. Not that I would ever lower myself to his level by going public with it, but sex with Blake was less fulfilling than my alone time with my battery-operated bullet. He could seriously learn a few things from Abe.

"Perfect!" Cyrus exclaims, pulling me back into the shoot. "In that last shot, your smile was so brilliant it could have lit up a city in a blackout," he tells me as he looks down at the camera in his hands and scrolls through the images. "I think we're done for the day, guys. Great work!"

"Thanks," I tell him as I break away from the group of men. I give a wave to them and say, "Bye guys. See you tomorrow," before I hightail it out of there. The hairs on my arms and the back of my neck finally relax as soon as I'm clear of the room and see Abe standing with his back holding up the wall.

"Finally finished?" he asks when he looks up and sees me, pushing away from his position.

"Yep. Let's go home," I say on a sigh.

"Hell yes," Abe replies while cracking his knuckles.

I debate telling him about the odd feeling I had after he left but figure I'm just being ridiculous. "I just need to change really quick," I say as I go over and turn the doorknob for my dressing room.

"I'll come with you," Abe offers, following close behind me.

"You can stay here," I tell him with a grin before I disappear inside.

CHAPTER TWELVE

Abe

MY RESTRAINT FOR NOT TOUCHING MERCY IN ALMOST FORTY-eight hours is wearing incredibly thin. It wouldn't take much for me to snap. Sleep deprivation isn't helping me rationalize shit either.

Seeing her around all those guys has me wanting to remind her that, despite their pretty-boy looks, they won't ever be able to make her feel as good as I can. And why is that? Because I would stay on my knees with my tongue between her sexy legs forever if Mercy asked me to. It wouldn't be a hardship either. It would be a goddamn honor.

"Stay here and lock the door," I order Mercy as soon as we walk through the front door of her house. I want to check every room and window first, making sure that there's no psychos lurking around. Nothing looks out of place, so I return to give her the all-clear.

"Thanks, big guy," she replies with an appreciative smile before she turns around right there in the foyer and gives me her back. "Would you mind unzipping me?"

Would I mind unzipping her? Um, fuck no.

I'm behind her a second later, grabbing the tiny zipper of her dress with my thick fingers and tugging it right on down. I start to ask her how she would've gotten out of the dress if I hadn't been around and realize exactly what's going on here. She's coming on to me, right? I could be wrong. So, to find out for sure, after the zipper stops at her lower back, as far down as it goes, I reach for the sides of her dress still along her shoulders and peel the material off of her until it puddles at the floor around her feet. And fuck me, she's going braless, only wearing a purple lacy thong that matched the dress she wore today. Which makes me wonder if she was wearing any panties at all under that white dress for the photos. Believe me, I would've seen the purple strings through that one. That's how hard I was staring.

Mercy hasn't moved or even breathed since I took off her dress. She's still facing away from me with her arms hanging by her sides, waiting. Waiting for me to make the next move. All that shit I told myself about not getting distracted while watching out for her psycho stalker goes right out the fucking window.

Stepping up against her, so that the growing bulge behind my zipper is pressed into her ass cheeks, I slip a finger into the elastic and run it back and forth from one of her sides to the other.

"Were you wearing any panties under the white dress?" I ask as I watch a shiver run through her body at just the motion of my finger along her lower back.

"No," she answers softly, making my finger pause in its movements.

"No?" I repeat in disbelief. "You were just strutting around with that pretty, red pussy uncovered?"

"Yes," Mercy replies, her voice barely above a whisper.

"Then why did you put on this sexy thong under the purple dress?" I ask. Pulling my finger back, I let the elastic pop her ivory skin. It leaves a red mark on the center of her lower back that I then soothe under my fingertips before letting them dip down to the crack of her ass.

"So...so that you could maybe take them off of me?" she replies like it's a question.

"Me?" I ask in surprise. "You wanted me to take your panties off of you?" My fingertips keep following underneath that string of her thong down, down, down until I feel the heat coming off of her pussy and they're coated in her sweetness.

"Ah!" Mercy exclaims and goes up on the toes of her high heels, the only other thing she's wearing, when I start petting her pussy, rubbing back and forth along the slickness of her lips.

"I asked you a question," I remind her.

She gasps a few more times before she says, "The other day...you said to take everything off...except my panties."

"That's right," I agree, rewarding her with a circle of my fingertips on her swollen clit that invokes a mewling noise from Mercy. "Because I wanted to be the one to take your panties off. I wanted to reveal this hot, little pussy slowly the first time so I could savor it."

Using my left hand that's not currently in between her legs, I tug the left string of her panties down, then the right, until they fall to the floor.

"But now that I've memorized the look, the taste, and the feel of this pretty pussy, I want your panties to be the first thing that comes off next time. That way I can give it a kiss even faster."

Next time? Did I seriously just say that?

"*Ohh,*" Mercy moans as I press the pad of my thumb against her tight opening.

"You do want me to kiss your pussy, don't you?" I ask her.

"*Yes!*" she cries out as her hips begin to swivel with the movements of my fingers on her clit and my thumb fucking her. "*Please!*" she begs as her body sags against the front of mine. My left arm locks around her stomach to hold her up while my right hand gets her closer to coming.

"I'm hungry," I whisper to her before I let my tongue trail along the shell of her ear. "How much of your sweet honey do you think I could eat?" I ask her. When a whimper is her only response, I give her the answer. "Every single drop I can wring from you."

"*Abe!*" Mercy screams as both of her hands grip my arm that's banded around her waist and she trembles violently with her release. My thumb is locked down tight in her slick canal as her walls spasm and pull it deeper into her body.

After the trembling from her orgasm finally subsides, Mercy's legs go so weak that I can barely keep her upright. Lifting her by her waist, I haul her over to the sofa and sit her down on it. She's as boneless as a ragdoll slouching on the cushions as I kneel down between her legs and tug her pussy to the edge.

Like she's being electrocuted, Mercy's back arches up and she screams at the first touch of my tongue lapping up her juices. I work my way from the outside of her lips inward where I nod my head up and down to drag the stiff tip of my tongue back and forth over her clit.

"*Yesyesyes!*" Mercy chants. Both of her hands come down on my head and her fingers spear through the sides of my hair to tug desperately on the roots while her hips begin to undulate against my face. The small hint of pain only urges me on until Mercy's thighs tense against my ears and then she screams my name with her orgasm. I keep licking her all the way through the shudders until her fingers finally relax in my hair.

Pulling back, all I can do is look at the beautiful woman laid out before me slumped on the sofa cushion. Her eyelids are lowered, cheeks and chest flushed red, breasts jiggling from her panting breaths and her pussy glistening from my handiwork.

My cock is trying to burrow its way out of my denim because it wants to be inside of her so badly, but at the same time, Mercy looks too relaxed and sleepy to take me just yet. So, while I wait for her to recover, I kiss the inside of her knee and up her thigh.

"Aren't you gonna fuck me now?" Mercy eventually asks, sounding half drunk or sleepy. "I mean, do you want to?"

"Do *you* want me to fuck you?" I ask with a smile while my lips keep kissing her mango-flavored skin and my beard rakes over her flesh.

"Yes."

"How?" I ask her while working two fingers into her pussy to get her ready for my cock.

Her eyes shut on a gasp.

"How do you want me to fuck you, Mercy?" I ask her.

"Rough," she says, making my lips and my fingers pause so that I can make sure I heard her correctly.

"Rough?" I repeat. "You sure about that, Red?"

"Yes. Just never gentle," she answers.

"Then I better add another finger," I tell her before I slip three inside of her, making Mercy's mouth fall open in a silent moan. "You do remember how big my cock is, right?"

"God yes," she moans.

"My size and rough sex don't really go together," I warn her.

"Fuck me like...like I'm a dirty, little slut who needs to be punished," she replies with a lopsided grin that makes me chuckle.

"If you say so." Lowering my eyes, I watch my hand disappearing as I pump three fingers in and out of her pussy a few more times. When I remove them all the way, Mercy whimpers.

"But you have to take your clothes off first," she adds when I reach down to undo my pants.

"If you want me naked, then you have to strip me," I tell her as I get to my feet. I quickly untie my boots and tug them off to give her a head start. Mercy tries to lean forward and reach my shirt, but the sofa is too low for her to push the tee up any further than my belly button. So what does she do? She holds on to me as she pulls herself up until she's standing on the cushions, making her just a few inches taller than me. With my hands on her hips to keep her steady, she easily pushes my cut down my shoulders and gets my shirt over my head. I release my grip on her long enough to pull my arms free.

I hear her loud gasp of surprise before I see the worried expression on her face.

"What happened to you?" she asks as her fingertips lightly graze the bruise the bullet left on my chest.

Looking down while I think of a lie, I say, "Nothing. Just got hit by a baseball."

"Baseball?"

"Chase has a wicked fastball."

"Yeah right," she says with a roll of her eyes. "The truth?"

"Bar fight," I hedge, but it's closer to what really happened. I just leave out the part about bullets and knives being involved.

"That I can believe," Mercy says before she leans forward to place a soft kiss over the center of the bruise and her lips starts making their way lower. My stomach tightens with warmth at her gentleness, and with anticipation.

When her mouth reaches my belly, her hands start working on unbuttoning my jeans, her eyes lowered and focused on the task of unzipping them and shoving them down. Mercy goes down to her knees on the sofa to follow them along to my knees, which means that her face is staring directly at my long, thick cock that's so hard it springs up and slaps my abs. Giving her a little help, I step out of my pants and remove my socks so that I'm standing completely naked in front of her, other than the ink covering my right arm and the Savage Kings patch tattooed on my entire back.

Mercy wraps both of her small hands around my dick and starts jerking me off. While it feels good, I'm more than ready to get to the part where I fuck her like a dirty, little slut, starting with her mouth.

Gathering up all of her hair in one of my hands at the back of her head, I use my other to cover her hands on my cock and then guide the tip to her parted lips.

When her green eyes lift to mine in question, I tell her, "Dirty little sluts suck a lot of dick."

She lets go of my cock, so I feed it into her mouth, loving the way her lips have to stretch just to fit the first few inches.

"How much can you take?" I ask, and she closes her eyes and moans around the fullness that's invaded her mouth. "The answer is as much as I give you," I tell her, keeping her head still with her hair in my hand while I thrust my hips forward. Right when I reach the back of her throat, Mercy swallows; and I nearly come right then and there.

"Jesus," I groan as I withdraw my shaft so that just the tip is in her mouth. She sucks on my dripping head so hard my eyes slam shut, and I see starbursts behind my eyelids. I have to grit my teeth to keep from slamming my cock down her throat and ending this blowjob right now.

"Mmm," Mercy moans as she slurps and drools on my dick. Her hands go around to my ass where her fingernails dig in and encourage me to thrust into her mouth. And I do, three more times before I have to jerk on her makeshift ponytail to pull her mouth off me before I come.

"Don't stop," she says when she looks up at me with her red, swollen lips and emerald eyes pleading for me to fill her mouth again.

"I'd rather come in your pussy," I tell her. "Turn around and lift your ass for me."

Nodding, Mercy quickly moves, positioning her face and chest on the sofa cushion with her legs spread, her ass raised in the air on the edge of the cushion in offering to me. And, fuck, am I ready to take.

Cock in my hand, I dip my hips to line up with her entrance, rubbing myself through her wetness before I finally push inside.

I fuck her like a savage, one hand squeezing her hip to hold her in place while the other jerks on her hair hard as I thrust in and out. Mercy cries out each and every time my cock bottoms out inside of her.

And despite what people may think when they see me, rough fucking is not my usual style.

With the clubhouse sluts, all I have to do is sit back and let them suck and fuck me however they want. They're so damn eager that I don't have to do anything but enjoy myself. Which is great and all most of the time, but sometimes I want to be the one calling the shots and taking control, just like right now with Mercy. The bizarre thing I can't figure out is that, if anyone deserved to be fucked slow and sweet, it would be her; but that's not how she wants it from me.

I don't last very long, not after her teasing me with her mouth and how tight and wet her pussy is after my tongue fucking. In record-breaking time that I'm not proud of, I bury myself as deep as I can go to let my hot release fill her up.

Fuck. I didn't use a condom again. That's twice now that I've been an idiot.

"Ohhhh....god," Mercy pants underneath me. I may have finished, but I haven't found the strength to pull my cock out of her yet.

"You sure that wasn't too rough?" I ask after I brace one hand on the back of the sofa to catch my breath. She may have changed her mind about what she asked for after I gave it to her so hard.

"No," she answers when she looks over her shoulder at me. "I love it rough. Don't ever do it any other way."

Fuck, I like the sound of that since she's implying that we're gonna be getting naked together again. But she's also making it clear that what's going on with us is nothing but a hookup. In the two times we've been together, I haven't kissed her lips even once. I'd think I was an asshole for not laying one on her, but Mercy apparently doesn't want anything but filthy sex from me. This woman isn't anything like I expected when we first met.

I finally have enough energy to push up from the sofa and pull out of Mercy's pussy. The mixture of our fluids come rushing out, making me wince.

"Next time I'll use a condom," I assure Mercy.

"It's okay," she says before she reaches around to dip her finger into the stream and then put it in her mouth. Watching her suck on her finger is enough to nearly make me come again. It's the sexiest thing I've ever seen in my life, and now I sort of regret pulling her mouth off of my cock earlier.

"Damn, woman. Now I want to be inside of that mouth again," I tell her.

"Later, big guy," Mercy replies as she climbs off the couch and stands in front of me, naked except for her heels. Reaching up while her deep green gaze holds mine captive, she cups the side of my face in her hand before rubbing it over my beard. "You look tired," she says before her fingernails rake down my chest to my stomach. "Didn't sleep much last night?"

"Not really," I admit as my abs tense and roll, trying to impress her.

"Then why don't you go and take a nap in my bed?" she suggests.

"I'm supposed to be watching out for you," I remind her. "I shouldn't have fucked you. What if the psycho had come in here while I was naked and inside of you weaponless?"

"You have weapons?" she asks.

"Yeah. There's always a gun in my cut and a knife on my belt."

"Oh," Mercy says as her eyes lower to my pile of clothes on the floor, making me sort of regret that honesty.

"It's just for protection," I explain. "I wouldn't hurt you."

"I know that," she says when she looks back up at my face. "It's actually pretty hot."

"Hot? Really?" I ask.

"Yeah," she answers. "And now I'll feel even safer while you're sleeping."

"I'm not –"

Putting her finger to my lips, Mercy says, "The house is locked up tight, and I'll wake you if I need to."

Since I figure that I'll need to sleep a little now to stay up tonight – the most likely time for someone to be creeping around her house – I eventually cave.

"Okay," I agree. "But don't leave the house and don't let me sleep for too long. Oh, and Reece will be coming by when the security system gets in, so don't answer the door for anyone who isn't wearing a Savage Kings cut."

"No problem," she agrees before giving my chest a push. "Now go sleep."

"Hard to leave when you're standing here in front of me naked," I point out with a smirk as my eyes dip to take in her breasts.

"Go!" she orders with a point of her finger down the hallway.

I'm not sure how much longer I can stay on my feet, especially after that incredible fucking.

"Night," I tell her. When I lean in to kiss her mouth, Mercy turns her cheek at the last second, so I kiss it instead.

Gathering up my clothing in my arms, I pad through the house until I find her bathroom. Once I clean up, I crawl into her bed still naked, sucking in deep breaths of Mercy's sweet mango scent before I finally drift off to sleep.

CHAPTER THIRTEEN

Mercy

IT DOESN'T TAKE ABE LONG TO PASS OUT. JUST A FEW MINUTES after he went to my bedroom, I followed him to put on some comfy clothes and round up my laundry to wash. He was already asleep on his stomach, taking up more than half of the bed with only a hint of covers draped over him from the ass down. I got a nice view of the large, black tattoo that takes up most of his back – the Savage Kings words along with their bearded skull wearing a crown just like the patches on the back of his cut. It's meant to be a scary, intimidating image anyway. So, on someone as big and muscular as Abe, it's a little terrifying at first. But I'm not afraid of him, even if he does have a gun. If anything, he makes me feel safe just being here in the house with me, even if he's unconscious.

The faint ringtone of my phone snaps me out of my perusal of the sleeping biker lumberjack, so I tiptoe out of the room with my clothes hamper to grab my phone from my purse. No surprise, it's Sasha.

"Hello?" I answer.

"Hey, girl. How are things going? Any more stalker notes?" she asks in concern.

"Nope. Abe is a pretty effective deterrent," I answer with a smile.

"Oh, I bet," Sasha agrees. "Has he been good for anything else?" she asks.

"Maybe," I give in to her curiosity as I lift my shoulder to hold the phone up to my ear while heading to the laundry room that's next to the kitchen with my hamper. "He's having a nap right now."

"A nap?" Sasha asks. "You're telling me that the big, bad biker is napping like a toddler?"

"Yes," I reply with a giggle. "He didn't sleep much last night."

"Well, it wasn't because there was any hanky-panky going on, right? Didn't he sleep on the sofa? What's up with that?"

"I-I dunno," I say as I pull my dresses from the hamper and put them in the washer. "And while I know I'm not supposed to be... dating while filming the show, that's not really what we're doing."

"Right, because you're just fucking, or so you say," Sasha replies.

"That's right, we are," I agree as I dig around in the hamper looking for my white zippered undergarment bag. It's the easiest way to wash all my bras and panties in the machine without them getting messed up. Who has time for handwashing each one separately? It's bad enough that I also have to line dry them.

"Sure. For now," Sasha adds while I keep hunting through the hamper. "But sometimes just fucking turns into more..."

"Sometimes. Not always and not in this case," I say, and then heave a frustrated sigh when I reach the bottom of the hamper without finding my bag.

"What's wrong?" Sasha asks.

"Nothing," I tell her as I straighten. "Just trying to wash a load of clothes but can't find my laundry bag. It must still be in my closet."

"Oh, okay," she says before, "So, you know we could totally double date now..."

"We're not dating!" I remind her with a roll of my eyes as I head back to my room. Lowering my voice when I'm outside the bedroom,

I say, "Even if we were, I wouldn't be allowed to do so with Abe in public."

"You could just not do the show," she suggests.

"I have to do the show. We start shooting tomorrow, and I need the money."

"Fine, whatever. They don't have to know about Abe being more than your bodyguard."

"Right," I agree before I say, "Okay, now I have to go and finish my laundry."

"Have fun!" she tells me.

"I'll try. Talk to you later," I say before we hang up. Placing my phone on top of my dresser, I tiptoe over to open my closet doors to see if the garment bag fell out into my rows of shoes lined up on the floor. I remove all of them from the closet, and still I can't find the damn bag.

Ugh, it's so frustrating. Where the hell did a week's worth of underwear go? I just put my sports bra and panties from my run in the garment bag this morning before we left. It's not like the whole thing could just get up and walk away...

Panic floods me when the only other possibility hits me – someone came in and stole them.

No way. That's...that's gross and preposterous! What kind of creep would do such a thing?

Oh, god.

A creep who leaves me twisted notes saying that I'm his soulmate and digs through my garbage maybe?

How sick can someone be to do that?

Yuck, yuck, yuck.

I refuse to believe he somehow got into my house and took my belongings. That's impossible with Abe around. None of the windows or doors were opened or he would've told me, right?

For the next half hour, I search every room in the entire house for my garment bag before I finally admit the truth to myself.

All of my dirty panties and bras have been stolen.

...

Abe

I WAKE up with my nose filled with the sweet scent of mangos.

Wow. I don't know how long I was out, but I slept like a big dog in Mercy's bed.

Blinking my heavy eyes open, I'm surprised to find her in bed with me. But it's not in the good naked way.

Mercy's sitting on the bed next to me fully clothed in sweats with her knees raised and her arms wrapped around them. What's most worrisome is her face. There's a blank thousand-yard stare that's directed toward the wall.

"Hey," I say, and just that one syllable causes her entire body to jerk like I've startled her. Her eyes squeeze tight as she blows out a breath as if to settle herself down. "What's wrong?" I ask even before her emerald eyes finally open and meet mine.

"Wh-why would you think something is wrong?" she asks, not denying that there *is* in fact something wrong, but wanting to know how I figured it out.

Sitting up on my elbow to get a closer look at her, I tell her a lie instead of the truth – that her eyes are wide and she's practically rocking herself back and forth like she just saw a ghost. "Random guess."

Taking a deep breath in that makes her chest rise underneath her tee, she exhales and says at the same time, "Myintimatesaregone."

"Huh?" I ask since she said it so fast, running the words together so that I didn't catch it.

"I can't find my bras and panties. The, um, recently worn ones."

My brows draw low as I try to comprehend why she's so upset about missing clothes and shit while I'm still waking up. Is that a chick thing? I'll have to ask Chase.

"You probably just misplaced them," I tell her.

Mercy shakes her head violently in disagreement. "No, Abe. I've looked *everywhere* for hours. They're gone – an entire weeks' worth!" she exclaims. Then, softer, she says, "I think...I think *he* stole them."

Fuck!

I pop up straight in the bed when I finally understand what she's saying. Her creepy ass stalker stole her panties and bras! "That sick son of a bitch!" I roar. The thought of some random asshole touching her delicates is just wrong. "When? When did he come in here?" I ask as I look around the room again for anything out of place.

"Sometime after we left this morning," she answers.

Shit. He came in while we were gone today? Or while I was fucking her? Dammit, I knew that was a bad idea, and I did it anyway!

Throwing the covers off of me, I jump out of bed and start getting dressed, putting my shirt, cut and jeans on before I pull out my cell phone.

"Who are you calling?" Mercy asks.

"Reece," I grumble. "This is his fault. If he would've been here this morning with that fucking security system, this wouldn't have happened!"

"He's already been here," Mercy informs me, making me freeze.

"You're kidding," I reply. "He came? Reece was here?"

"Yes. He set everything up and said to call if I had any questions about how the keypad works or whatever," she says.

"Reece was here? In the house? While I was fucking sleeping?" I exclaim, then end the phone call. Looking out the window, it's completely dark. How long was I asleep?

"Why are you yelling at me?" Mercy asks, still sitting in the same spot with her arms around her legs. "You asked him to come by to install it..."

Stabbing my fingers through my hair to give it a tug, I say, "I should've heard him. How did I sleep through that shit?"

"You were tired," she answers even though I was mostly asking myself the question. "And he wasn't here very long, just an hour or so..."

"An hour or so!" I shout. Two or three minutes is all it would take for that bastard stalker to come in here and hurt her. The fact that I left her unprotected for hours is unacceptable.

"It's fine, Abe."

"It's not fucking fine," I disagree with a shake of my head as I sit down on the edge of the bed to put on my socks and boots.

"Where are you going?" Mercy asks.

"I need to check the system," I tell her as I pull on one of my boots, then the other. "And I need to keep an eye out on the front and back yards..."

"I'd rather you stayed in bed with me," Mercy says. "Some sick bastard stole my underwear. I'm scared, Abe."

Fuck, I hate hearing her say that shit. Getting to my feet, I turn to tell her, "I'm gonna be either outside or in the living room..."

"Will you please just...just hold me?" she asks softly.

"I can't," I reply. "I can't do that and be a half-decent bodyguard. Earlier today was a mistake. A distraction that could've ended up with you hurt."

"But it didn't," she replies.

"No, it didn't that time, but it could the next time. That's why there won't be a next time," I assure her before I walk out of the bedroom.

CHAPTER FOURTEEN

Mercy

THE NIGHT AFTER ABE FUCKED ME INTO OBLIVION, SOMEONE stole my dirty panties, and then Abe flipped out for no reason after Reece came by and installed the security system, I'm in hair and makeup for almost two hours. Which does my self-image no good at all, especially when the makeup artist sounds like my mother, telling me I should get more sleep and put cucumbers over my eyes to help with the swelling. How do I get sleep when I have a crazed stalker out in the world and the one person who makes me feel safe refuses to touch me?

Abe made it clear that nothing will happen between the two of us again, basically stating that having sex with me is just a distraction that he doesn't want or need.

I'm so over the whole fantastic sex with him. Or so I tell myself.

Now, it's time for me to finally get to speak to the twenty handsome bachelors on the show.

Once the sun went down, the crew set up filming in the driveway of the oceanfront mansion with the waves crashing in the background and the moonlight reflecting off the ocean. The lights lining the driveway and sidewalk to the front of the house glow warmly, inviting guests inside. It's beautiful and romantic, yet all I can think about is the brooding giant standing off to the side, watching me like a hawk with his arms crossed over his thick chest.

He's tired again and should've given up his sentinel services hours ago to get some sleep, but of course he refused. I don't know what Abe is going to do since he can't possibly stay awake twenty-four hours a day, seven days a week until we're able to identify and catch my stalker.

"Mercy, the first bachelor is ready if you are?" Ryan, the producer of the show, says from where he's standing next to one of the cameramen.

"Sure," I agree as I look down and smooth my hands over the front of my long, black gown to make sure everything is in place. Since it's strapless, I'm worried that too much movement may cause my breasts to pop right out the top.

"Everyone quiet on the set. Cameras ready. Let's pull the limo around, and action!" Ryan shouts.

I plaster a smile on my face when the headlights of the black limousine first appear before it drives up and comes to a stop right in front of where I'm waiting at the entry of the sidewalk. The passenger side nearest me opens, and then out steps a tall, lean, dark-haired man that I recognize from the photoshoot. His smile is enormous as he buttons his black suit jacket and approaches me.

"Hi, beautiful," he says in greeting. "I'm Roman."

"Hi, I'm Mercy," I reply with a grin.

When he holds out his arms for a hug, I step forward to give him a quick embrace since it's expected. And he's tall, almost as tall as Abe, but not nearly as big and muscular.

"I can't wait to get to know you more," he says when the two of us separate.

"Me too," I agree. Still smiling, he nods and then continues up the sidewalk toward the house where all twenty bachelors will be living together during the filming. That is one part of this season that I definitely won't miss. The majority of the show is based on the drama that happens in the house during the competition. When you put twenty men, or in my case last season, twenty women, under one roof, there will always be fireworks.

The limo pulls away and then drives back around the semi-circular driveway a moment later to drop off a different man.

"Hiya, babe. I'm Tanner," the next guy, a man who has ear-length light blond hair says. Even before he called me babe I wasn't interested in the surfer boy. No, the only thing that was even slightly appealing were the tattoos that peeked out of his orange, yes, orange, button-down and cuffs. I had no idea that I was so attracted to ink, not until I met Abe...

Eighteen men later and I've finally met all of the contestants who I'm supposed to get to know over the next four weeks before I finally choose my soulmate. But deep down in my gut, even after meeting them for just a few seconds each, I already know that none of them are Mr. Right. I hugged all of them, and none of them even sparked the smallest warmth in my chest or in my lady parts.

The only names out of the twenty that I remember are Brian, Tanner, Roman, Henson, Robert, Cale, Eric, Winston, and Zeke. The only reason that I remember two of those names, Henson and Eric, is because they were assholes. How could I judge that based on a smile, greeting and quick hug? Well, the entire time both men only looked at my cleavage and not once at my eyes.

After all of the initial introductions, the crew sets up inside and on the patio for me to go mingle with all of the men.

I'm supposed to be learning about what they all do for a living, their hobbies, etcetera, but really it makes me feel like I'm back in the elementary schoolyard with boys fighting over who gets to have a turn on the swings. I'm the swing in this scenario, and I don't really want any of them. They fight over who can get me a drink, a refill on my wine, who gets to talk to me alone, and I even hear a few whining about how I didn't spend as much time with them as so-and-so.

Also, it's incredibly difficult to act like I'm having a one-on-one conversation walking with a man on the beach when I know that Abe is watching and listening from just a few feet away.

There are just too many guys to keep straight, so hours later when it's time for me to deliberate on who I want to send home, I have to sort through photos with the producer to figure out which two I want to send home tonight along with the perverts, Henson and Eric.

Is it crazy that I want to ask Abe his opinion?

I wonder who he would pick, or would he tell me to send them all home? I ultimately decide on two more photos of men who could barely think of a sentence to say to me all night because they were also too busy looking at my breasts.

The ceremony involves me handing out red heart pins for the men to each wear on their shirt collars or lapels. When all the pins are gone, I tell the four standing with the group who did not get pins that I'm sorry, but they did not win my heart, so they must go home. Cheesy, I know, but the show *is* called *Queen of Hearts*.

Once I give the boot to the perverts, dwindling the group down to sixteen bachelors, the producer finally says it's a wrap for tonight.

Tomorrow, the real fun will begin with competitions for the guys to win a solo dinner date with me.

Abe is sitting in a lawn chair with his arms crossed in front of my trailer, looking about as thrilled as a man waiting for a root canal. It's surprising that he hasn't inserted toothpicks in his eyes to hold them open since it's so late.

"Ready to get out of here?" I ask him.

"I was ready to leave the moment we got here," Abe grumbles, then yawns. "It's almost two fucking a.m."

"You've been awake for way too long," I tell him when he stands up and stretches his arms over his head, revealing a hint of his tan stomach. "Are you hungry?" I ask, since he needs to eat before I insist that he sleeps.

"Hell yes," he agrees. Can't say I'm surprised either. Big men need a lot of food.

"We can grab breakfast, and then you're going to sleep," I tell him on the way to my car.

"We'll see," he answers grumpily.

After Abe gets some bacon, eggs and pancakes in his stomach at the local diner, he becomes a little less hostile. His eyes finally meet mine again between bites, and the scowl behind his beard seems less severe.

"What did you think of the show?" I ask while I finish eating my fruit salad.

"Ugh," Abe groans. "None of those fuckers are good enough for you."

"Really?" I ask.

"Oh yeah. All of them are total pussies. At least you got rid of the pervy ones fast," he says.

"You noticed that too, huh?" I ask. "They were only interested in having conversations with my boobs."

"No shit," Abe gripes. "I wanted to gouge their eyeballs out."

"Thanks for not doing that," I tease him. "The producer probably would've had to find more men, and that could've taken forever."

Abe's phone that's sitting on the table buzzes, and some sort of notification pops up on the screen before he quickly drops his fork to grab it.

"Fuck," he mutters.

"What?" I ask.

"Your porch camera just had movement," he tells me, causing the food in my stomach to nearly revolt.

"Maybe it was a cat," I say, trying to be hopeful.

"Nope," Abe disagrees before he turns the screen to show me. It's a still photo of a man in dark clothes. He's wearing a baseball hat that casts shadows on his face so that only his eerily glowing eyes show up. He looks like he's trying to peek into my front window!

"Holy shit," I mutter as a shiver runs through me. Abe and I could've been home, in bed asleep, while some creep tries to look at us or get into the house.

Tossing his phone down on the table, Abe says, "This is why I can't fuck you or fall asleep."

"Is that the only reason?" I ask softly so that the late-night owls around us won't hear.

"The only reason what?" Abe asks when he picks his fork back up to spear some fluffy eggs.

"That you don't want to...you know, have sex with me," I whisper.

"I can't risk the distraction," he says. "This fucking stalker is serious if he's stealing your panties and lurking around your house in the middle of the damn night."

So, I'm a little disappointed that he still thinks sex with me is a distraction. Even so, he can't go without sleep. "You have to rest sometime," I point out. "And I would feel much safer if you were resting in the same bed as me. Isn't there another option?"

Abe pauses in his eating for several long moments while his dark eyes watch me. I brace myself for his rejection yet again.

CHAPTER FIFTEEN

Abe

I'm so damn tired. I don't know if I've ever been as exhausted as I am right now.

And horny. I'm really fucking horny, but mostly I want to pin Mercy down and make her forget about all the assholes she met on that stupid show today. All the fuckers who got to touch her when I haven't laid a finger on her since yesterday afternoon because I'm trying to protect her.

And I can resist her body right along with sleep. Or at least I could, until she had to go looking all gorgeous and pitiful when she said that she would feel safer with me in her bed. Dammit, I want to be in her bed, and I want to watch over her.

But I can't do both fucking things at the same time.

That's why I'm unable to believe the words that are coming out of my mouth when I tell her, "Mercy, I think we need to call the police. The fucker's gone too far. Digging through your trash was one fucking thing, but it's not illegal. This shit, though? He's breaking and entering and creeping around your house at night. There's no telling what he's capable of."

"You...you think we should get the police involved?" she asks, emerald eyes wide in surprise.

Fuck, she's gonna make me admit to the bitter words again.

"Yes."

If my brothers could hear me, suggesting that she notify police, they would slap me upside my head.

"I don't want there to be any articles about this..." Mercy starts to say.

"That would suck if it happened," I agree. "But you're in danger, and I'm only one man."

Goddamn, I hate admitting aloud that I don't think I can protect her. I'll do everything in my power to keep her safe, but I can't stay awake on alert every hour of the day. What if he comes in when I'm sleeping or when I slip up and fuck her again? I can't take that chance. Because I will end up inside of Mercy if she'll let me, despite how stupid it is. And for some reason, I want to fall asleep with her in my arms, knowing that she's safe.

Since I don't know the local police, I'll first call in a favor with Chase and Torin's stepsister, Jade, who is also our new sheriff up in Carteret County. Pulling out my phone from my zippered cut pocket, I text Chase and ask him to send me Jade's cell phone number. Since it's the middle of the night, I don't expect a response from him for a few more hours. That's why I'm surprised when my phone buzzes from beside my plate a few bites of my breakfast later with a message.

Wincing with worry that I may have woken him up, I pick it up and read the message.

What's going on? Give me a call and I'll put Jade on the phone since I'm with her right now. She went into labor earlier tonight and just delivered my niece, Makayla Engle.

"Shit," I mutter. While I'm happy for her, now is the worst time to bother Jade with the stalker mess if she just gave birth.

"Everything okay?" Mercy asks as I hold my phone. It starts ringing before I can type back to Chase to tell him never mind, since they have their hands full.

"Chase, sorry to bother you so late and when you're busy," I say into the phone.

"Abe, hey, it's Jade," the feminine voice replies. "What did you do?"

"Nothing this time," I answer. "And congrats on the baby. This can wait," I tell her. "Everyone doing okay?" I ask, since it seems like the polite thing to ask. Across from me Mercy's brow is furrowed in confusion.

"The baby and I are both doing great. With an epidural, there was nothing to it, and now my adrenaline is up, so tell me what's going on."

"Are you sure?" I ask.

"Yes! Start talking. I'm curious as to what crime you've committed now."

"Fine," I mutter when I cave. "But I really haven't done anything. I'm calling for...a friend," I say after a long pause trying to figure out what Mercy is to me. Guess we're sort of fuck buddies, but I didn't want to call her that.

"Okay, what's going on with your friend?" Jade asks.

"She has a stalker," I start, then tell her about the letter and catch her up to the missing underwear. I hear Chase and Sasha corroborating the story in the background.

"Are you sure she didn't just misplace them?" Jade asks when I'm finished. "Women lose clothes all the time..."

"No, she's absolutely sure. I'm guessing based on her level of concern that she went over every inch of the house looking for them. This guy is dangerous. He showed up on the security camera tonight too."

"Jeez. Sounds like he could be a real basket case," Jade agrees. "And you're sure you want me to call this in to the local PD?" she asks, knowing that with my criminal record and with the MC's stance on law enforcement that we don't like to involve cops in our business.

"I'm sure," I tell her after quickly weighing the pros and cons again. Even though I hate asking for backup, I think it's necessary to put a squad car on Mercy at all times to ward off the psycho. I thought me being with her would be enough to scare him away, but now I'm not so sure. And being wrong on this could hurt Mercy. I won't take that chance. Our prospects and my MC brothers have more important things to worry about right now with looking for Hector and shit. I can't ask them to follow me and the woman I care about around all day when Torin needs his retaliation more.

"Okay. Give me the address and I'll have WPD send someone over right now tonight to file a report."

"Thanks, Jade," I tell her before I rattle off the info. "We're eating breakfast but should be home in about half an hour."

"I'll tell them. See ya, Abe," Jade says before ending the call.

"Chase's stepsister is a sheriff, so she's gonna get someone from the local PD to come by the house and get a statement," I explain to Mercy, who gave up on eating her girly fruit shit.

"Okay," she agrees with a nod.

"You're going to be okay," I assure her, reaching over to give her hand a squeeze.

"I know. It's just, he's violated my privacy and he thinks he loves me, but I don't even know who he is. That's the scariest part," she says before her eyes dart around the restaurant. "It could be anyone."

"Yeah, it could," I agree, looking around to see if anyone seems suspicious. Most of the customers are in pairs or groups of three or more except for an ancient old man at the counter who looks like he could barely walk, much less stalk someone. "That's why it's best to have more eyes on you everywhere you go to make sure you're safe. I don't want to let you down."

"Thank you," Mercy says to me before she lifts my hand. Kissing the center of my palm, she places it on the side of her face as if seeking comfort from me. And while I've never comforted anyone before, it seems like it comes as easy to me as riding my bike.

...

Mercy

I HURRY into the house when Abe finally allows me to get out of my locked car to enter it.

"Reece said he looked inside and then gave up and left," Abe tells me when we're both standing in the living room with every light on. "And I've checked every inch."

"I know, and I appreciate it," I tell him, wrapping my arms around myself protectively. "It's still just sort of creepy being here now..."

A knock on the door nearly has me jumping through the ceiling.

"It's probably the cop," Abe says in explanation. "Go and stay in the bedroom while I check the door."

"Okay," I agree with a nod, walking that way with him behind me.

In the brightly lit room, I watch as Abe pulls something out of the inside of his vest. "Mind if I leave this here in one of your drawers?" he asks, holding up a big freaking gun. "I'm not supposed to possess one."

"S-sure," I say, pretending that I see guns all the time and it's not a big deal as he opens the bottom dresser and then slips it inside before strolling off down the hallway.

Am I surprised that Abe basically just admitted that he's a

convicted felon who isn't supposed to own a gun? Yes, and I'll have to ask him about what he did soon. But I still trust him just as much.

I hear my front door open and then the mumbled conversation between two men before heavy footsteps grow louder in the hallway. Abe appears in the doorway with a small, young man in a blue uniform trying to see around him.

"The officer is here, and he needs to get your statement," Abe tells me.

"Okay, sure. Should we go in the living room?" I suggest. It feels weird sitting or standing in my bedroom while talking to a police officer.

"Wherever you're most comfortable," the officer says as I walk toward the door.

"The living room is fine," I say as I squeeze past the two men and lead the way.

I take a seat on the sofa, where Abe immediately joins me. He throws his arm around the back of the sofa, not touching me, but close enough that I can feel his warmth.

The officer's eyes flick rapidly between the two of us for several silent moments before he says, "Ma'am, would you be more... comfortable doing this down at the station?" His gaze goes back to Abe and then me again with a raised eyebrow. Apparently, he thinks Abe is my problem.

"It wasn't Abe," I assure the officer. Getting up, I retrieve the letter from the stalker that I folded and put in my purse, then hand it to him. "I got this letter after the first night that Abe was here. Whoever left it was jealous of Abe."

Again, the officer's eyes go to Abe, as if worried he may jump up off the sofa and attack him, before he finally begins to read the letter.

"Can I keep this for the file?" the officer asks.

"Yes."

Pulling out a small pen and paper from his shirt pocket, he starts taking notes while still holding the letter. When he's finished, I go through the details of my missing underwear, and then Abe shows him the photos from the security camera that were taken earlier tonight.

"Is there any way that you can keep this off the record or out of the media?" I ask the officer when he's finished taking notes. "I'm getting ready to shoot a reality TV show, and this is sort of private."

"Sure, ma'am," the officer says. "But I think you need to have one of our squad cars close by at all times until we find the culprit. Our department has actually done this before for celebrities who are in town. We can get in touch with your production team, and they can make the arrangements to pay to have a black and white assigned to you."

"Understood," I reply. "If anyone asks, I'll tell them that the escort is for paparazzi, which isn't exactly a lie. They're starting to get out of hand."

"The department will be glad to help you with that as well. Having an official escort can be more effective than, um...private security," the man says with a smile until Abe clears his throat in a threatening way.

"Got everything you need?" Abe asks when he stands up from the sofa as if to remind the police officer that he's twice his size.

"Yeah, I, um, I think so," the cop says before he finally starts walking toward the front door. "I'll write this up outside and take the first watch until seven a.m."

"I really appreciate that," I tell him as I follow him. "And Abe does too, even if he won't say so."

"Are the tags on this bike up to date?" the cop calls out as he starts down the sidewalk and is next to Abe's Harley.

"Hell yes," Abe mutters in response from behind me.

"Just checking," the man says before he climbs into his marked cruiser.

I shut the door and lock up behind him.

"So now will you finally agree to get some sleep?" I turn around and ask Abe.

In response to my question, Abe only growls before he picks me up, tosses me over his shoulder and carries me to the bedroom. "There's something we need to do first before I get some sleep," he says before he tosses me on the bed and follows me down. My legs automatically part for him to wedge his big body between them.

Abe looks down at me for several long seconds with his brow furrowed, a frown partially hidden by his thick beard.

"What's wrong?" I ask him when I run my fingers through the sides of his hair. "I mean, other than my psycho stalker."

"I've never kissed you," he says before the corners of his lips lift into a grin. "Well, I have on the lower parts of your body but not right here." Lowering his head, Abe softly brushes his lips over mine. It's sweet and gentle, totally unexpected from the big tough guy. The problem is I like it a little too much. I can't afford to let feelings get wrapped up into what the two of us are doing. Sex without emotions involved is incredible with Abe, and I don't have to worry about getting my heart broken if I don't put any expectations on him.

"Tomorrow I start filming," I warn him, speaking the words against his lips.

"Yeah, okay," Abe agrees before his damp lips immediately lower to my neck.

"I can't...date anyone while filming the show," I explain further even though it's becoming incredibly difficult to think clearly with his mouth making my entire body tingle with expectation.

Finally, Abe lifts his mouth to look down at me. "Does that mean I can't fuck you?"

"No," I reply quickly, because I'm not ready for us to stop doing this together. "Just that no one can find out."

"Chase and Sasha know," he points out.

"Well, no one other than our close friends," I clarify. "To everyone else, you're my bodyguard, nothing else."

"Okay," Abe easily agrees, as I expected, and then the bottom of my shirt is covering my face and a tickly beard is moving down my stomach, ending all further conversation.

CHAPTER SIXTEEN

Abe

MY LIFE IS TURNING INTO ONE BIG ROUND OF DÉJÀ VU.

It's the second night of filming, and this one is even more brutal. I had to watch eight assholes take turns dancing with Mercy before she picked one who got to have an hour long private dinner with her.

Maybe I'm biased, but the guy was goofy as fuck and only talked to Mercy about chess for the whole meal. Chess, for sixty minutes. There's no way she would want to be with someone that damn boring, right?

I don't ask her, though, in case I'm wrong. Instead, I stay quiet on the drive to an open all-night diner like the one we ate at yesterday, the police cruiser following behind us the whole way.

It was while we were waiting for our food that Reece sent me a text nearly identical to the previous night, some motherfucker looking in Mercy's damn house.

"That's it," I grumble when I get to my feet.

"What?" Mercy asks. Before I can respond, she says, "He's there? Again?"

"Yes," I answer, hating the panic in her eyes that one word causes. "I'm gonna go talk to the officer outside, see if they can send someone over to the house right now, because I don't want to leave you."

"I don't want you to leave either," Mercy says instantly. "Have the police send someone."

Nodding, I leave the table and push open the glass door to step outside. When I walk up to the police cruiser with my phone clenched so tightly in my hand the case starts to crunch, it takes a moment for the cop to roll his window down. He looks a little nervous when he finally does.

"There's some asshole at her house right now," I tell him before I show him the screenshot of the photo Reece just texted to me. I'm starting to wonder if that man ever sleeps either.

"Shit," the officer curses. "I'll call it in and have someone circle the neighborhood. Is the suspect in a vehicle?"

"Not that we know of," I say before texting Reece to ask him. "If my IT guy monitoring the cameras finds out more, I'll tell you."

"Thanks," he says before he rolls the windows up.

There's no fucking way I'm taking Mercy back to her house tonight. I know I won't be able to sleep, and I doubt she will be able to either. Last night neither of us got any rest until the sun came up, partly because I couldn't keep my hands or mouth off of her, but mostly because we were both a little paranoid.

When I retake my seat at our booth, Mercy blurts out, "I don't want to go home tonight."

"Good," I say with an exhale. "I was thinking the same damn thing."

"Should we get a hotel room?" she asks. "It's too late to wake up Sasha and Chase."

"Nah, we don't need a hotel or to bother the lovebirds," I assure her. "We can stay at the clubhouse."

After a few weeks, we've finally been able to plaster and paint over all of the bullet holes in the doors and wall. The bar is officially open to the public again with more security cameras out front and inside. We learned our lesson after Hector's attack, so now each of us have no less than three firearms locked, loaded and ready in all of our apartments, in the chapel, and behind the bar. It's an incredibly safe place, so I know Mercy will be fine with me there.

"Okay," Mercy agrees. "Tomorrow, we can go by the house for me to change clothes before we have to be on set."

"Yeah," I agree, even though I'm dreading having to endure another day of men gawking at her while imagining fucking her. I know that's exactly what they're thinking, because no straight, single man can possibly look at her without it crossing his mind. And while I may not be good enough for her, I don't think any of those bastards are either.

After we eat and I pay the bill despite Mercy's protests, I give the officer a heads-up that we're going to the clubhouse and that he needs to park on the street. My brothers would lose their shit if they saw him on the lot.

"That's out of my jurisdiction, so I'll call the Carteret sheriff," he replies. That's fine with me, since I would prefer that one of Jade's officers shadows us. Besides, they're on the MC's payroll.

Our hour ride up the highway to Emerald Isle is silent, filled only with the music Mercy puts on while I drive her car. I finally break and ask her about what I saw on the set earlier.

"Do you like chess?" I ask her.

"Ah, no," Mercy answers.

"So that guy..."

"He's definitely going home tomorrow night during the ceremony," she tells me. And when I glance over, I can see her smile even in the darkness.

"Good," I reply. And while it's a relief to know she wasn't into that dork, I can't help but wonder if she's into some of the guys. I fucking hate that shitshow. I've never been jealous of other men. Hell, I've shared most of the girls that hang around the clubhouse with at least one of my brothers, and it's never been a big deal. The whole MC could fuck Cynthia and I could watch without a single spark of jealousy.

But thinking of Mercy with anyone else makes me want to snap some necks.

Even just thinking about bringing her into the clubhouse has me on edge. I don't want any other male to look in her direction. I want her all to myself – her body, her smiles, her laughs. They're mine, and I'm not fucking sharing them.

After we park and I calm myself down from the ridiculous jealousy, I unlock the door to the bar that's now closed while trying to picture what everything would look like from Mercy's perspective. I'm glad that none of the women I've fucked are around. Not because I don't want them to meet Mercy; but because, as crazy as it sounds, I feel like a bastard for sleeping with them before I met her, like I was preemptively cheating. It's stupid, I know, since we're not even together but just screwing each other.

Entering in the code for the basement, I hold the door open for Mercy to go first down the well-lit stairs, and then I show her to my small apartment. My hands that are trying to unlock the door are actually shaking because I'm so nervous about her seeing my space. I've never been nervous before; the clubhouse sluts don't give two shits what my room looks like. They follow me down because they want to fuck. Mercy, though, I want her to like my personal area, so I hope it's not too big of a mess. We have a housekeeper Reece hired who comes and cleans up trash, washes our clothes, and even washes our sheets for us once a week. Otherwise, the entire place would be a pigsty. Oddly enough, I've never seen the woman who does the cleaning. She's like a fairy maid who swoops in and tidies up without us ever noticing her.

"I know it's not much, but I just sleep here," I say to Mercy as I push open the door and flip on the light, realizing that my worry is more about her thinking I'm poor and shit since she's so classy.

"I can't wait to see your place," she says with a grin before she goes inside and starts looking around.

The first spot her eyes land is on the desk that's covered in junk.

"What's all that?" she asks while I close the door and lock it behind me.

"Nothing," I answer, looking over the dusty antique clock along with several watches and ancient electronics with the wires hanging out. "Just some crap I'm trying to fix."

"You're gonna fix all of this?" Mercy asks, walking over to take a closer look.

"I'm gonna try to," I reply.

"Will you keep it all? Are you a collector?" she asks while glancing back at the room that's pretty much empty other than the furniture.

"Nah. There's a pawn shop just down the road. I help out the old guy who owns it when he takes in crap that doesn't work. He's a sucker for a sob story."

"Oh," she says. "So you fix things for him? That's nice of you."

"Just trying to pay back a little of my debt to society," I mutter.

"What's that?" Mercy asks.

"Nothing," I tell her. What would she think of me if she knew I used to go around stealing people's shit just like her creepy stalker stole from her? I know I fucked people over, and at the time I didn't think I had a choice. It was either hurt strangers by taking their belongings or my brother and I would get kicked out on the streets where we would starve to death.

Ready to strip down for bed, I remove my cut and hang it up in the closet before pulling off my shirt.

"Can I sleep in that?" Mercy asks, eyeing my worn, black Motorhead tee.

Fuck yes, she can.

I toss the shirt to her. Although I would rather sleep with her naked, seeing her in a shirt that belongs to me is the next best thing.

"Thanks," she says as she pulls the material over her head.

We both meet in the center of the bed where Mercy says, "I'm so tired. Will you just hold me tonight?"

"You don't ever need to even ask, Red," I assure her as I wrap my arms around her and pull her closer to me. "The answer to that question is always yes."

"Thanks," she says with her face buried in my neck, allowing me to get a big whiff of the mango scent of her shampoo.

Honestly, I'm too tired to even try to fuck her tonight. There's always tomorrow or the next day. So, for now, I place a kiss on top of her head and drift off to sleep.

...

"Yo, Abe. Church in ten if you're here!" Sax yells through the door after he knocks on it, startling me and Mercy both awake.

"Go back to sleep," I murmur to her as I rub her hair to calm her down. It's probably late in the morning, but she needs the sleep even more than I do. Once she relaxes and is settled back down, I ease out of her grasp and cram my pillow in her arms instead. The way she squeezes it to her chest and presses her face into it makes me regret my decision to leave. But the truth is, I may not be around the club much for the next few days. I need to drop in on a meeting to catch up on everything, especially Hector.

I take a fast as fuck shower, pull on a clean pair of jeans and a tee over my still damp body, and then grab my phone to check the time on the way out the door. It's only eleven, so maybe I can get a few more hours of sleep with Mercy after our meeting.

Locking my apartment door behind me, I head down the hall where Sax is holding the phone bucket. I toss mine inside and give him a nod before entering the chapel. All of my brothers are already sitting around the table except for Torin, which isn't surprising. I lock eyes with my brother, Gabriel, to see how he's holding up. He seems good, so I jerk my chin up in a greeting that he returns before Sax joins us after shutting the door.

"So what's up?" I ask as I take my usual seat on Chase's left. He may not have a Sergeant at Arms as VP; but if he did, I know I would be his man.

"We've got a hit on Hector's daughter," he says solemnly before his usual smile bursts free. "She's in Vegas, so who's up to pop in and say hello after we have a fucking wedding?"

"Yeah!" the whole table roars in agreement.

"Congrats, man," I tell him with a clasp of my hand on his shoulder. Chase and Sasha have wanted to elope for over ten years. It looks like fate is finally letting them get their chance.

"I'll let Sasha handle all the arrangements, so whatever date she sets is when we'll fly out. We need to go ahead and figure out who is staying and who is going," Chase says.

"I'll stay behind," Reece offers, which is no surprise since he's a homebody. "No offense to the bride or groom."

"None taken," Chase agrees with a grin. "We need a few men to stay behind and hold the place down."

"I'd love to go, but sitting on a plane for hours is damn near impossible with these old knees," Eddie declares.

"Understood. We'll need you to help run the salvage yard and probably the bar with Turtle."

"Done," Eddie agrees with a nod.

"You know I won't miss out on your wedding," I tell Chase.

"Good," he agrees. "War and Cooper, you want to come along to keep an eye on Torin?"

"Fuck yes," Cooper agrees.

"I'm in," War agrees. "Just need to make sure my sister can babysit."

"Of course," Chase agrees. "Sax, Dalton, Gabe, Miles, it's up to you four to decide if you want to go or stay."

"I don't want to miss a trip to Vegas," Sax replies with a grin.

"Me either," Dalton agrees.

"I'll stay," Gabriel declares. "Too many appointments scheduled over the next few weeks. It would be impossible to reschedule them all. Congrats, though, man. I wish you and Sasha the best."

"Thanks," Chase replies. "Miles?"

"I'll stay here," he answers. "Not supposed to leave the state since I'm still on probation."

"Then we definitely don't want you to get locked up for a bull-shit violation," Chase agrees. "And can you check in on Ian while we're gone, see how he's holding up and if he needs anything other than a few more Playboys?"

"I can go see him," Gabe offers excitedly, which makes sense because Ian was his sponsor when he was prospecting, so he's pretty tight with Ian just like I am with Chase. I know he's missed the man these last few months. "I mean, if that's okay with Miles?" my brother adds.

"Good man," Miles agrees with a tip of his chin in Gabe's direction. "I always worry the fuckers won't let me leave once I walk through the prison doors."

"So, we've got it all settled except for the two prospects. Leave them here or take them?" Chase asks.

"Maddox is coming up on a year. So, if he wants to go, I'll keep an eye on him," War says since he's the kid's sponsor.

"Good," Chase agrees. Looking to Cooper, he asks, "What about Holden?"

"I think you should keep him here," Coop responds. "He's a little hot headed, causing bullshit problems at *Avalon* when he's supposed to be there helping me and Miles out with bouncing. We don't need to draw any attention to ourselves in Vegas. Well, no more than our cuts will get us when we're on the other side of the country."

"Very true," Chase replies. "Talk with me more about him later."

"Will do," Coop says.

"I'll fill everyone in as soon as I have the dates lined up with Sasha. Until then, unless my brother specifically asks, let's try and keep him out of the loop. Only because Torin is raring to go, and we need to do a little more surveillance on the girl and make plans before heading off half-cocked. All we know right now is that she applied for a driver's license. Reece tracked down the address she listed on it, but it's for a resort, not a house. We need a little more time to locate her."

Everyone expresses their agreement with him.

"Next up on the agenda," Chase says. "Why the *fuck* is there a pig sitting outside our parking lot?"

"Oh, that would be on me," I admit, and everyone looks at me in concern, especially Gabe.

"There's no heat," I assure them. "It's for Mercy."

"You brought her here?" Chase asks with worry in his voice.

"The asshole showed up to her house again last night. Reece has a few images of him, but I'm guessing he was probably gone by the time the police got there. We haven't heard anything from them so far."

"Damn," Chase mutters. "You could've brought her to our place."

"I know, and I appreciate that, but it was around five a.m. by the time we had breakfast. We didn't want to wake you and Sasha, and you had a late one the night before with Jade."

"Understood," he says. "So, she's got the police escort now?"

"After we realized he broke in her house and keeps coming back, it was pretty much the last resort," I explain.

"Jesus. Well, let me know if either of you need anything," Chase says.

"Will do."

"Then we're done here," he says, reaching for the gavel and slamming it down before dropping it right away as if he can't stand to touch the thing in Torin's absence.

"So, what's this about some girl you brought here?" Gabriel asks when he comes up to me. "This your old lady you were talking about the other night?"

"She's not my old lady," I assure him, even though I wish she were. "She's Sasha's friend, and she's got a stalker. I'm making sure he doesn't fuck with her."

"Sounds like it's more than that. You said she made you want to be a better man or some shit. That's deep, man," he replies. "So, are you gonna let me meet her or what?"

"Yeah, of course," I tell him. "She's asleep right..." I start to say before I hear catcalls and whistles from out in the hallway where most of our brothers are leaving.

I hurry up behind them and push my way through to see exactly what they're losing their shit for. Of course, it's Mercy; she stepped out of my apartment wearing nothing but my t-shirt.

"Red, get your bare ass back in there!" I shout at her while pointing the way in case she forgot in the two steps she took from the room.

"I missed you," she says while tugging on the bottom of my shirt, even though it comes down past her knees.

"Yeah, well, miss me in my room or with some more clothes on," I gripe, even though I can't actually be mad at her. How could anyone, as beautiful as she looks without a shred of makeup on and her red hair all big and sexy from being tousled in sleep on *my* pillows in *my* bed?

"Damn, Abe," Dalton comments first. "She the one you trying to put on the shot? Give that shit up, man. You better put a baby in her before I do."

"Shut the fuck up," I warn him, not liking that thought at all. "All of you need to move the fuck on!" I suddenly roar. My anger from seeing Mercy with all those guys on set, as well as my frustration with this stalker shit gets unleashed on my brothers, who are now gawking at her.

When the entire hallway goes deadly silent, I realize I may have overreacted. But dammit, I'm tired of everyone looking at my woman and trying to get in her absent panties. That's my pussy, and I don't want any other dicks going near it.

Silently, everyone finally disperses either to their rooms or up the stairs, except for Gabriel.

"Hi, I'm Abram's brother, Gabriel," he says to Mercy, who is still standing in the same spot, refusing to follow my orders. Seems like she only follows the ones that involve us getting naked.

The two shake hands, and Mercy even smiles up at my brother. She looks at me briefly and says, "Abram, huh?" probably since I never told her my full name. "I'm Mercy Daniels. And you two definitely look alike. The eyes and dark hair for sure. Love your ink," she adds, pointing to the tattoos on his neck and all the way down his arm.

"Thanks," he says proudly. He may not have tatted the black and white skulls and dragon designs on himself, but he did draw them.

"So my brother is helping you out with a stalker?" Gabriel asks.

"Yes," she answers, glancing at me again.

"Well if you have any problems with Abram stalking you, or ever need some ink, just let me know." He even pulls out one of his business cards and hands it to her.

"Thanks, Gabriel. I definitely will," Mercy agrees with a smile before I pick her up and drag her back into the room with my arm around her waist after a gruff goodbye to my brother. He and I can sometimes go months only grunting at each other, but then he gets all chatty with my girl that he just met.

CHAPTER SEVENTEEN

Mercy

I WOKE UP CLUTCHING A PILLOW TO ME THAT SMELLED LIKE Abe. For a split second, I panicked when I realized he wasn't in bed, but then I remembered we're in his apartment at the MC's clubhouse and that he's probably close by. I opened the door to take a quick peek...and found a hall full of tough-looking men in leather heading right for me. Since they had all stopped in their tracks, it didn't seem polite to just slam the door in their faces. Besides, I wanted to see how Abe would react, if he would introduce us or treat me like I was just a random woman he was sleeping with.

Now I'm trying to figure out if he always looks like he wants to kill the men who look at the women he's fucking.

I don't have a chance to ask Abe; because as soon as he hauls me into the room and shuts the door, he's bending me over the bed and ripping his shirt off of me. At first, I have no clue what he plans to do to me, not until I suddenly feel his tongue between my thighs, which his hands spread wide. I cry out in surprise and in ecstasy. Abe knows how loud I am, so does he want the other men in this place to hear me screaming his name?

Apparently he does, because after the first time I shout his name in gratitude for making my body tremble with pleasure, I'm rewarded with a smack to my ass. It's not hard enough to hurt, so I'm pretty sure it's a reward for giving him what he wanted.

Once his fingers penetrate me, though, I say so long to the English language and become fluent in mind-fuckish. Abe doesn't give me any warning before his cock slams inside of my wet, throbbing pussy and takes me higher than I've ever been.

When Abe's quick, hard thrusts finally end with a long grunt, neither of us move, even though most of his weight is pressing me into the mattress. The sounds of our heavy breathing echoes loudly in my ears.

"Sorry," Abe eventually says.

"For what?" I ask through the pants. "Your talented tongue, fingers, or cock?"

He's silent a moment before he answers with a short chuckle. "All of the above, along with the ass slap."

"It's okay," I assure him. "It was great. Every second. Just not sure what I did to deserve it."

"You were too gorgeous to be standing in our hallway wearing nothing but my shirt," he replies.

Smiling even though he can't see it, I ask, "Are you always so... possessive with your other beard riders?"

"Hell no," he grumbles. "I've watched my brothers fuck most of the same girls I've been with and never gave two shits."

Ew. Do they really do that? "You guys...share?"

"Oh, yeah," Abe answers before he finally moves off me so that my lungs can fully expand again. He stretches out on the bed on his back, and I force my weak limbs to crawl further up the mattress so that we're face to face. "The girls upstairs are community property. They know that when they walk through the door," he informs me.

"Would you share me?" I ask.

"Fuck no," is Abe's instant response before his brows furrow. "Why would you ask me that? Is that what you want?"

"No," I answer honestly. "Just wondering why you would share the other women but not me."

"Because you're better than all of those girls put together," he says. "And because I don't want another man to take my place."

"As my bodyguard?" I ask, to see if he'll answer the question about what we are exactly. We're not dating, so we're either fuck buddies or friends with benefits.

"Yeah," Abe answers simply. I wait for him to give me a more detailed explanation of our brand new and somewhat odd relationship, but he doesn't even after several silent minutes. I guess that means he doesn't think we're doing anything more than fooling around.

"Can I, um, use your shower?" I ask to break the silence.

"Go for it," he replies.

Scooting off the end of the bed, I grab Abe's shirt I was wearing before he discarded it and head for the adjoining bathroom, even more confused. Why I thought he may want more than to just sleep with me, I'm not entirely sure. But at least now I know the score.

...

TODAY ON SET, there's a competition for the sixteen remaining guys. In four heats, four men are supposed to jump into the mansion's pool, swim to the other side, grab one of the dummies that each weigh as much as I do (which is incredibly embarrassing), then swim back with it and pull it out of the water. The one with the fastest time wins a private dinner date with me. The dummy represents me, of course; and this little contest is supposed to show me which man I could count on to rescue me if I were drowning.

I cheer on each heat as the guys struggle to haul the heavy dummy while trying to stay afloat. It's sort of funny to watch them putting the dummy in a headlock, or some even trying to lie on top of it, using it as a floatation device.

Between the first two heats, I make the mistake of glancing over behind the scenes to Abe. Of course, his eyes are on me. Noticing me locking gazes with him, he arches one dark eyebrow as if to say that he has no doubt that he could win a race against these chumps. After they're all finished, I just may let him give it a go.

The winner of the challenge is Zeke, a former high school swim team captain. His time is right around two minutes and forty-five seconds.

"I can't wait to take you out tonight," Zeke says as he stands in front of me in nothing but a speedo. All the guys had to wear one so that the female viewers could get a good look at their very athletic, very sculpted bodies. Zeke's floppy brown hair is still dripping wet. So, when he flips it back, I get sprayed with the chlorinated water in my face. Zeke, of course, laughs before he starts apologizing. He grabs a towel and starts mopping up my face while the camera captures every second of the exchange between us.

"Hopefully we'll both stay dry during dinner," I tell him.

"We'll see," he remarks with a suggestive wink before he heads back over to the line of men, who are pouting because they didn't win today's event.

"Next time, guys!" I shout to them before I wave goodbye.

"And that's a wrap for now," Ryan, the producer, says. "Gentlemen, you can all get back to the house. Zeke, get showered and put on your dress clothes. Mercy, you'll need to change into an evening gown. I'll have Randy bring over a few choices, but I'm thinking blue is your color tonight."

"Yes, sir," I agree.

Abe strolls over toward me; and when he's about three feet away, he starts removing his cut. It hits the ground, and then he pulls his shirt over his head.

"What are you doing?" I ask with a laugh.

"Time me," he says with a nod of his head toward the pool.

"Abe, seriously?" I ask, glancing around at all the people still hovering around us. But then Abe is untying his boots to take them and his socks off. I gasp when his jeans come down. Since he's not wearing anything underneath, I end up staring at his big, swinging cock for way too long before I remember that we have an audience and the prudent thing would be to shield my eyes. "Abe!" I yell at him.

"Are you filming this?" I vaguely hear the producer ask the camera man, and see that they're following Abe around the pool where he grabs one of the dummy dolls, throws it over his shoulder and then carries it naked to the other end of the pool. Once it's in place, he goes back to the starting side.

"You timing this?" Abe asks as he points to someone behind the scenes. Apparently, they give him the go ahead, because he dives into the water a second later and quickly crosses the pool. One of his big hands reaches up to grab the dummy by the leg, and then he's swimming back, only a little slower because he's using just one thick arm. At the wall, he tosses the dummy up and then pulls himself out of the water, flashing all of us his tan ass.

"Two minutes and twenty-one seconds," the timekeeper calls out. Abe pumps both of his arms in the air to celebrate his victory, making me laugh. And while he may not have won a romantic dinner with me tonight, there's no doubt that he just won a pretty good consolation prize for his incredible feat of manliness – my mouth until he fills it with his release.

Grabbing a towel from the stack, I walk over and hand it to him. "You should probably cover up King Kong before he scares everyone."

"Ha!" Abe chuckles. "So, what did I win?" he whispers as he wraps the towel around his waist.

"Guess you'll have to wait and see," I reply vaguely before I reach up and squeeze the water out of his beard. The way I'm fisting it is no doubt similar to a way I would hold something else and milk it.

"I'm not a very patient man," he says.

"Don't worry, it'll be well worth the wait," I tell him.

"Ah, Mercy," Sofie, one of the set techs, calls out to me. "Your mic is still on."

"Oh, right," I say, feeling my cheeks flush. I try to replay our conversation back to see what it would sound like to someone listening. It must have been somewhat naughty if Sofie felt the urge to warn me. Hopefully she won't share that recording with anyone else, or I'll be screwed.

CHAPTER EIGHTEEN

Abe

"OH, FUCK, YES, RED," I GROAN AS MY DICK DISAPPEARS INTO Mercy's wide-open mouth.

Unable to remain standing, I tug on Mercy's hair to pull her forward as I walk back, keeping my cock in her mouth until I'm able to take a seat on the side of my bed. It's almost midnight. We just got back from recording her fucking date with the swimming asshole on the show that I beat, and I need her mouth to make me come so bad I can't stand it.

"Suck me, suck me, suck me," I chant as she does just that, moaning and bobbing her beautiful, red head like she can't get enough. The only problem is that I can't see enough of her. As soon as we got to my room, she was unzipping my pants; and that's as far as either of us got. Now I want to see her gorgeous body. Grabbing the front of her thin summer dress with both hands, I jerk on either side of the material until it shreds down the middle, baring all of her to me, including her pussy since she gave up wearing panties and bras except for the ones on set after some of hers were stolen. While I hate that fucker for doing that to her, I have to say that I'm happy as hell that she's decided not to wear any more to avoid feeding his sick obsession.

"Rub that pretty pussy for me while I fuck your mouth," I tell her, and she does it right away, lowering one hand between her thighs and touching herself with two fingers. The sounds she makes around my cock while pleasuring herself have me even closer to blowing my load.

While I had planned on letting her get my dick wet with her mouth before I fucked her, that plan is slowly fading away the longer she's on her knees.

"I'm gonna come," I warn her through gritted teeth when it's impossible for me to hold off any longer. Her response is to take me deeper into her mouth, so I give up the good fight and give her everything I've got. Mercy swallows what she can before she pulls back and finishes me off with her hand. She closes her eyes and lets my hot bursts of pleasure land on her face.

And, fuck, it makes me feel like an asshole for treating such a beautiful, classy woman in such a vulgar way. When I finish, I fall backward on the bed with my hands behind my head to stare up at the white speckled paint on the ceiling. From the corner of my eye, I see Mercy get up and go into the bathroom to clean herself off.

When she comes back in the bedroom, I feel the mattress dip when she climbs up on it. And then, she's curling up beside me with her head on my chest while fingernails slip under my shirt to graze up and down my stomach.

"Why do you let me fuck you like that?" I ask her.

"Like what?" she replies innocently, even though I'm sure she knows what I mean.

"Like a dirty little slut or whatever you called it the other day."

"Because I like it that way," she says. "I like how you aren't afraid to be a little rough and dirty with me, unlike the other men I've been with."

"You shouldn't be treated rough or dirty," I tell her.

"Why not?" she asks. "If that's what I want and what you like too? It's hot. At least it is for me..."

"Yeah, it's hot," I agree. I've never come as fast as I do when I'm with Mercy. So why do I feel guilty when I do the same thing to her that I've done to other women?

Because I care about her and don't want her to be like the others – nothing but a good time and then it's over.

"What's wrong, big guy?" she asks.

"Nothing," I respond. It's not like I can ask Mercy to quit the show after they've started filming it. She just met me. And, for one reason or another, I'm not the type of man she thinks is "Mr. Right." Mercy's just slumming it with me, the convicted felon and outlaw, because the sex is great. In a few weeks, she'll have to pick a guy. And once her perverted stalker is caught, she won't need me in her life. She'll go on to marry some banker or lawyer and have a slew of kids while I'll be still stumbling through life like I'm not sure where I belong.

...

OVER THE NEXT FEW DAYS, I watch jealously from the sidelines while lesser men flirt and carry on with my woman. They compete in more events with each other to win alone time with Mercy. My least favorite would be the one where she's blindfolded and has to try and guess which man is which based on nothing but running her hands over their faces, arms, chests and stomachs.

Despite the stupid candlelit dinners and shit, at least I know that every night I'm the one who gets to take Mercy to bed and fuck her. Afterwards, I hold her for a few minutes before she falls asleep and rolls away from me.

That part at the end of the day is what gets me through the torture of seeing her surrounded by other men. Oh, and I fucking love when she sends guys packing, eliminating them from the competition.

Too bad I can't be whatever kind of man it is that she's looking for. I try to figure out exactly what that is while I watch from behind the scenes as the contestants are dwindled down to four.

Is it because they're pretty boys? I'm not exactly hideous, I don't think.

Are they rich? Probably, but Mercy doesn't seem like she cares about money all that much. Even though she has no clue, I actually have a decent sized bank account.

Is it my size? I'm bigger than the other men for sure, not just in height but more muscular too. Does Mercy prefer small men? Nah, I doubt that.

So, I guess all I'm missing is the part where I don't ever want any kids or have the brains that these four last men standing have. The fuckers all told her they want lots and lots of kids. Also, they definitely had me on the giant crossword puzzle thing they had to complete with only Mercy's favorite things as clues. I knew them too; it just took me a little longer to fill in the board with letters once the show stopped filming.

The truth is, I dropped out of high school when I was fifteen, the year our mother killed herself. Since Gabriel was only thirteen, he went into the foster system without me. I went to the streets instead because of my juvie record that no one wanted to deal with. Before, I had been stealing food and smalltime shit to feed us and give Gabe gifts for Christmas and his birthdays. But after our mom died, I started stealing cars for a local chop shop in Charlotte to get by while I tried to find out where my brother was living. Then, when I found him, I got busted and lost my freedom, leaving Gabe to fend for himself yet again. I made a stupid mistake, and I regretted it for the entire eighteen months I was locked up and all the years since.

Is my criminal record and stupidity the reason Mercy only wants to keep me around as her bodyguard and to fuck me until she finds the man she wants to marry? Being big enough to kick someone's ass and fucking are really the only two things that I'm good at. I know it, she knows it, and so does everyone else.

CHAPTER NINETEEN

Mercy

"Mercy, can I see you in my trailer for a minute?" Ryan, the producer, asks after we finish shooting my last elimination before the finale. Only three men remain, Roman, Vincent, and Zeke.

"Sure," I reply before I quickly catch up to him before he gets to the steps of his trailer.

"Need me in there?" Abe asks when he suddenly steps in front of me before I climb the stairs.

"No, I'll be fine. Thank you," I say with a smile and reassuring pat on his arm.

And while I'm trying to play it cool on the outside, I'm so freaking excited that tomorrow morning we're all headed to the airport to fly to Vegas for Sasha and Chase's wedding. Not just because I'm her maid of honor, but because I'll get to travel with Abe. Thankfully, Sasha could wait a few days for the show's filming break so that I could join them.

Abe's dark eyes narrow in disapproval of me being alone with another man, but Ryan is great and I'm pretty sure he's gay, so he doesn't have to worry about me. Randy, his assistant, is usually by his side, just like now.

"Come on in and have a seat," Ryan says when I pull the door shut behind me.

He sits down on one side of the table, so I sit on the cushion opposite him while Randy hovers near the door, playing on his phone, ready to jump as soon as Ryan asks him to go fetch something.

"I wanted to talk to you about a possible extension on your contract," Ryan starts.

"Really?" I ask in surprise since we're taking a week break for me to make my decision, and then the show is over, other than the reunion episode that happens after the show airs.

"Yes," he replies with a smug grin. "Randy, where's that contract?" he asks his assistant, who quickly goes over and starts digging through a stack of documents on a side table. Apparently finding the right ones, he brings them over to Ryan.

"Thanks," he says to his assistant before he flops the papers down in front of me. "I've spoken to the three finalists, and each of them has also agreed to the extension in the event that you pick them in the finale."

"What would be the extension?" I ask, thumbing through the wordy documents that I'm too tired to read right now.

"So, I'm not saying that we would have to film the wedding, but we would want to film several months of you two living together, maybe starting to make some of the wedding plans. What do you say? I can offer you double the money from the show's original contract."

"Wow," I mutter since that is a lot of money. "But I would have to actually live with the man I choose?"

"Yes," he answers. "When the cameras are off, you could have separate bedrooms for all I care. While they're rolling, though, you would have to appear a happy couple in love, which means you wouldn't be able to date anyone for another six months or so."

"Six months?" I repeat. Sure, to most people that's not very long to have to be roommates. If that were all it was to it, I would sign the papers right now. But it's not. I would have to stop seeing Abe for good, or at least for six months. I could be wrong, but I don't think the big guy would wait around for me while I played house with another man for half a year. That is if he even wants to keep seeing me after the psycho stalker is caught. At least he stopped showing up at my house after the second night. Still, Abe and I have been driving back to sleep in his apartment instead of taking any chances. Sure, it's a little small, but it's cozy and I feel safe under the MC's protection.

"Your rent, utilities and all other living expenses would be covered," Ryan adds. "It's all in here," he says, tapping his finger on the top of the documents.

"This is a great offer," I tell him. "Could I have some time to talk to my agent and think about it over the break?"

"Absolutely," he agrees. "I will need an answer by the time we shoot the finale so that I can start making arrangements."

"Good, that should give me plenty of time," I say in relief. *Plenty of time to figure out what Abe wants,* I think to myself.

"Great," Ryan agrees. When he moves to stand up, I do the same, grabbing the papers up from the table to study later. "Any big plans for the week off?" he asks as we start for the trailer door.

"Yes, actually. My best friend is getting married in Vegas," I reply with a smile.

"That sounds like a good time," he says, then opens the door for me to leave.

"Yeah, I can't wait," I agree. As soon as I start down the steps, I see Abe waiting for me in the exact same place I left him. He's like a human statue. Sometimes I'm not sure how he stays so still and patient.

"See ya, Ryan," I say when I start to head back across the yard to cut through the production set.

"Have fun in Vegas. Just not too much!" Ryan calls out with a grin. "Cameras are everywhere!"

"What was that about?" Abe asks, eyeing the papers in my hand.

Rather than explain it before I even make a decision, I say, "Just contract stuff. No biggie."

Honestly, how things go with Abe on our trip will probably help me decide whether or not I agree to the extension. If he tells me that he wants more, then I would turn it down. I'm just not sure if he's the type of guy to *ever* want more. Sure, Sasha's man is in the MC and is settling down, but the two of them have been in love since they were teenagers. I really doubt that any of the other bikers are seeing anyone seriously.

...

Abe

I GET the feeling that whatever paperwork Mercy came out of the producer's trailer with is more important than she's letting on. I'm not sure why she dodged the question when I asked her about it, or why I go and snoop through her things when we get back to my apartment and she's in the shower, but I need to know what they say.

I gently pull the papers from inside her purse that's sitting on my desk and unfold them. Again, my lack of education catches up with me. It's a bunch of legal terms I don't really get, but going through the pages, it looks like they want Mercy to live with the man she picks at the finale for six fucking months.

Is she actually considering signing this horse shit and moving in with one of the assholes that have been fighting over her like little kids? I knew she had to pick someone at the end of the show, but I thought it would end there and then she and I could really be together. Not just in my bed, but out in the rest of the world.

If she's going to live with one of them, then there's no fucking way I'm going to stick around and watch that bullshit. It makes me think that I was right, and Mercy's only sleeping with me to take a walk on the wild side before she picks Mr. Right and settles down with him to start a family. There's even shit about their engagement and wedding in the damn paperwork and an insane amount of money for an additional extension if Mercy gets knocked up. The thought of her going off the birth control shot to fuck some douche bag from a stupid television show to have a kid makes my pulse start to pound throughout my entire body.

When I hear the shower cut off, I shove the papers back into her purse and try to calm my rage. It's barely in control when the bathroom door opens and Mercy steps out wearing nothing but a towel around her gorgeous body.

"As soon as we catch your fucking stalker, I'm done with you," I blurt out. "And I'm done sleeping with you. I can't do this anymore!"

"Abe, what are you talking about?" Mercy asks, coming over to lay a hand on my arm. "Did something happen while I was in the shower? What's wrong?"

"Everything's wrong!" I yell, jerking away from her and sitting down on the edge of my bed. "I can't fucking breathe when I see those fancy dressed limp-dick bastards drooling over you on that stupid show. I thought it would be over soon, but to find out that you're signing on for an extension, that you're going to shack up with one of them..."

"What?" Mercy interrupts me, looking over at her purse to see the papers I hastily stuffed in there peeking out. "Abe, that contract is just a proposal they want me to consider. Nothing is set in stone."

"Then why didn't you fucking tell me about it?" I yell, standing back up.

Mercy doesn't flinch or back down at all. "Because of this!" she yells back at me. "Because I don't know what *this* is, what we're doing. It's one thing to be bossy in the bedroom, but now you're going through my things? Why would you do that? I've had enough violations of privacy the last few weeks without you digging through my things without bothering to try and have an adult conversation about what's going on between us. Just because we're sleeping together doesn't give you the right!" She gets closer to me as her voice rises, struggling to keep her towel on as she stands toe-to-toe with me.

"And what *are* we doing, Mercy? You've made it pretty clear that I'm just the fuck-boy bodyguard that you're using for a good time, keeping me on the back-burner until your stalker is locked up and you find Mr. Fucking Right on your goddamned show!" I roar. "I know I'm not good enough for you, but I'm not going to stand around and be some pussy-whipped heartbroken runner up. I'm done with this. Go find your Prince fucking Charming and get the hell out of my life!"

"What are you talking about? You *are* good enough..." Mercy starts, before I turn my back on her and storm over to the door.

"I'm calling Sasha to come pick you up. Go stay with her until our flight to Vegas. You'll be fine over there. You two can compare notes on your pussy-ass husband candidates," I tell her, before I walk out and slam the door.

Once I'm outside, I have to lean on the wall in the hallway, waiting for the agony in my chest to ease. It feels like I'm having a fucking heart attack; it's too tight inside me to breathe. I have no idea what this feeling is, but I'm starting to think that bullet did more than just leave a bruise on me. It feels like my heart is...broken. I shake off that ridiculous thought and stomp upstairs and out the bar, flipping open my phone to call Sasha.

CHAPTER TWENTY

Mercy

AFTER ABE STORMS OUT, I FINISH DRYING OFF AND GET DRESSED while trying to replay everything he said in my mind. I'm incredibly pissed at him for digging through my purse and frustrated with how demanding the big, sexy brute is being. He knows that I have to work out this show's contract, or I'll be blacklisted from any other programs in the future. This extension wasn't my idea, and I haven't even had a chance to read over the papers yet, much less discuss it with him.

To top it off, he had to make a crack about being a heartbroken runner-up. He said he never saw that season of *King of Hearts* that I was on, but to take a shot like that at me...why doesn't he understand that I can't just put myself out there for him, after what happened to me before? I needed to know where his heart was, and I guess today I found out.

I go upstairs to the bar, knowing that Abe won't be there. None of the people who are milling around even pay any attention to me as I walk outside and wait for Sasha. I decide not to call her myself, hoping that Abe didn't do it and he'll come back. Only a few minutes later, though, her Mustang pulls into the bar parking lot, and she jumps out to come over and hug me.

"What happened? Abe called and just told me I needed to come get you!" Sasha says.

"I think we...I don't know. Can you break up if you were never together?" I ask her, hating the knot in my throat and the tears that finally begin to spill down my cheeks.

"Oh Mercy, no..." Sasha says, wrapping an arm around me and pulling me over to her car. "Come on, let me drive you to your house to get packed up for our trip tomorrow, and then you can come stay at our place tonight. Tell me what happened with Abe. What are you fighting about?"

Once I'm in the car, I show Sasha the paperwork detailing the new program I'm being offered. "They want to give me a new show, one where I live with the guy I pick from the *Queen of Hearts*. I hadn't had a chance to really look it over or talk to Abe about it before he dug it out of my purse while I was in the shower. Once he saw it, he got so angry, and told me we were done." I fish a tissue out of my purse and blow my nose, so I don't sound like I'm sniveling.

"That is one thing about the boys in the MC — they can be the jealous type," Sasha tells me.

"He said it was killing him, seeing me being pursued by the guys on the show," I confirm. "Doesn't it figure that this freaking show is the thing that's now ruining my love life?"

"Your love life, huh?" Sasha teases me. "So, tell me honestly, what's between you two? How do you feel about Abe?"

"I...can't say," I tell her, looking out the passenger side window so she won't see the lie in my expression. When I glance back over at her, she is smiling at me knowingly.

"All right, fine. I have...feelings for him," I confess to her. "But I can't do it, Sasha. I can't put myself out there like I did with Blake. He broke my heart, and he wasn't even..." I trail off as Sasha arches an eyebrow at me.

"Blake wasn't what, girl? Go on, spit it out." Sasha prompts me.

"He wasn't half the man Abe is. In any regard," I admit. "But that just means Abe could hurt me even worse if I tell him these things and then he keeps acting this way! If he wants me, really wants me, he's going to have to show me."

"Give him some time," Sasha says. "We're all going to be in Vegas for the next few days, and that city has a way of making wonderful and strange things happen."

I reach over to turn up her stereo, which thankfully ends our conversation for now. We ride the rest of the way to my house without any further conversation, but do sing along together when a Bon Jovi song comes on.

Once we pull into my driveway, I nervously get out of the car and stand at the foot of the steps leading up to my front door and the walkway to the beach.

"It's fine," Sasha assures me, "You haven't gotten any security e-mail updates since those last photos were captured, have you?"

"No, thank goodness," I sigh in relief. "He couldn't have been back around the house. And besides," I say as I nod to the patrol car that followed us from the clubhouse and just parked across the street, "I still have my escort nearby."

We climb the steps together and pause by the front door as I fumble for my keys. "My stomach still gets tied up in knots thinking about some freak being in here, digging through my underwear, you know?" I tell Sasha as I finally get the key into the lock.

Before I can step inside, Sasha grabs my arm and points over the long walkway attached to my house, leading down to the beach. I follow her finger and see that down near the outdoor shower, where my clothesline is hanging, are several items flapping in the ocean breeze. "We wouldn't be talking about *those* underwear, would we?" she asks.

"Oh no," I gasp, realizing that the security cameras only cover the corners of my house. The walkway extends almost fifty feet over the sand dune, well out of their line of sight.

"Don't worry, what's the worst it could be? The freak did your laundry?" Sasha laughs. "I mean, we'll have to burn them, but at least he brought them back and he's not in some basement wearing them on his head. Come on, no one is down there. Let's go take a look."

I start to protest, but Sasha is already stomping across the porch. Since there's an officer just across the street, I steel myself and follow her. Sure enough, my delicates are spaced out along the clothesline, my bras closest to the house.

"Oh, Mercy, my god, look at this," Sasha gasps. She pulls out her phone and points the flashlight on the letters written in bright red Sharpie along the splintered wood of the walkway.

"I CAN SMELL YOU"

"There's another one down there, by your panties," Sasha points out, and we grab each other's hand as we take a step over. In the same bright red ink on the rail underneath the rest of my intimates is written:

"I CAN TASTE YOU"

"Oh boy," Sasha mutters. "If that means what I think it does, I'm gonna be sick."

"Jesus, Sasha, the outdoor shower, the stall there!" I squeak, gripping her hand so tightly she flinches.

Sasha immediately ducks down with her flashlight, as the door to the stall doesn't reach the ground. Releasing an explosive sigh of relief, she says "No feet, don't worry. No one is lurking in there. Just in case, though," she says as she marches over to open the door.

"Don't!" I yell, but she's already thrown open the door. Sasha's hand flies up to cover her mouth as she steps back, then she turns to me in alarm. "Get in the house, right now," she says as she looks around warily.

"What is it?" I demand. Ignoring her order, I take the phone from her hand and move closer to peek into the stall. Written in the same ink, in huge letters that takes up the wall of the stall is the message:

"AND IF YOU LOOK UP...I CAN SEE YOU"

"What?" I gasp, looking around in a panic. "What the hell does that mean?"

Sasha suddenly gasps and grabs my arm, jerking me around and pointing over the rooftops of the nearby beach houses. There, a few houses down, one of the neighboring rentals has a large cupola on the roof of the home. A figure is standing there, only visible as a silhouette in the moonlight. A shimmer of light shines and glints from what I'm guessing are the lenses of a pair of binoculars he's using to gaze down on us.

Sasha and I both take a few horrified, tentative steps back towards her car, unsure if this is just a coincidence, until the figure raises one hand and gives us a jaunty, welcoming wave.

"Get your things," Sasha tells me. "I'll grab the cop and tell him that crazy bastard is right there, only...what is that, six, seven houses down? Go, girl!" she tells me with a light shove to get me moving.

Hair flying behind me, I dash into my house, digging under my bed to grab my suitcase and throwing clothes into it willy-nilly. I'm barely aware of what I'm packing, and I rake my arm across my vanity to dump my make-up and supplies on top of my clothes haphazardly. By the time Sasha runs back onto the porch, panting and out of breath, I'm already heading outside with my roll-behind luggage and my carry-on.

"Let's clear out of here, now," I gasp, winded from my whirlwind through the house.

"I'm locking the door. Go, go, go," Sasha says, shooing me out the door as she reaches inside to kill the lights.

The officer is no longer across the street as we throw my bags into the trunk of Sasha's car. "I told him what we saw, and he went down the street to check it out," she tells me. "He's going to come investigate the scene up here later, then call us. I told him we wouldn't need him to follow us out to the farmhouse, Chase will be there, and we'll be leaving soon for Vegas."

Once we're in the car and safely away from the house, I manage to catch my breath. "Do you think that officer will be able to catch him?" I ask Sasha.

"I wasn't able to give a good description of the guy we saw since it was just his silhouette," Sasha sighs. "The officer said he would check it out, but all the guy would have to do is walk down to the beach and disappear in the darkness. Don't think about that, though. They'll call and let us know what they find. Let's focus on getting out of town and away from all this craziness for a few days! We can stir up our own brand of crazy out on the Vegas strip, away from your would-be suitors and stalkers!"

"I wish…" I begin to say, before choking it off.

"You wish what?" Sasha teases me with a raised eyebrow.

"I just wish this was over, the show, this freak who is out there, all of it," I lie lamely.

"Uh-huh," Sasha agrees sarcastically. "Don't worry, those wishes will come true soon enough. And if you were thinking about wishing for a big, bearded biker-fellow, well, he will be along tomorrow, at the airport. Give him some space so he can get his head straight. Abe's mom was…not good for him, or his brother. The first woman he was supposed to love tore him apart and ruined his childhood, so he has trouble with all of them now. Kind of like what happened with you and Blake."

"Great, you didn't tell me he had mommy issues when you introduced us," I scoff.

"Not living in her basement, or not being able to cook or do his own laundry type issues," Sasha corrects me. "From what Chase has told me, she was a drug addict who left Abe and his brother alone when they were tiny, for days at a time before she overdosed and died. Abe would have to go out to neighborhood stores and steal anything he could to feed them. The only reason he's a felon is because he kept getting caught."

"He's a bit too big to be much of a thief," I agree. "Not really the profession for a man of his stature. Abe's not exactly inconspicuous. But wait, you don't get felonies for shoplifting, do you?"

"I dunno about that, but Abe did mention to me once that he got locked up for grand theft auto," Sasha informs me.

"Wow."

"Yeah, later on when his little brother was in middle school, Gabe showed a real talent for art. They needed clothes, supplies, you know, normal teenage stuff," Sasha tells me. "Abe already had a juvie record and couldn't even find a fast food job, and he didn't want Gabe following in his footsteps. He fell in with a group of guys who boosted cars, guys he had met while in the detention system. If his mother and her 'friends' hadn't constantly stolen from him, he might have been able to just do a few small jobs and get out, but he kept needing more cash. His luck finally ran out when he was eighteen, and he ended up doing some real time. He met Chase while he was inside." Glancing over to me she says, "Hey, don't let Abe know I gave you his sob story, okay? He wouldn't like it if I was telling you his business, at least not right now."

"Of course," I reassure her. "I'm glad you told me. It kind of explains, well, everything about him. I just can't wait to see him, though. Tomorrow can't get here fast enough."

"I'm with you there," Sasha agrees. "I've been waiting to marry my man for over ten years. This is going to be a great week, girl, for both of us. You'll see."

CHAPTER TWENTY-ONE

Abe

THE ROAR AND VIBRATION FROM MY HARLEY FEELS LIKE IT'S going to crack open my skull when I roll into the airport the next morning. Once Chase confirmed that Sasha had picked up Mercy, I went back to the bar and crashed in the corner, drinking and smoking until my guts started trying to crawl up my throat. A couple of my brothers tried to come talk to me and find out what had put me in such a dark mood; but after I sent a few scampering away with their tails between their legs, the rest understood I wanted to be left the hell alone.

The truth is I'm not entirely sure why I'm in such a shitty mood. Mercy has been nothing but an angel to me. And if it wasn't for this damned show she has to finish and the men she has to be seen with, I think I might have a chance with her. I know she's acting this out and has no real interest in any of those guys. The problem is that I just can't completely trust any woman not to destroy me. All the women that have ever come into my life have wanted to use me in one way or another, and the idea that she truly likes me for just being myself is hard to wrap my head around.

I leave my bike in the underground long-term parking lot and double check the straps on my carry-on, cinching it tightly to my back. Everything I need for a few days rolls up nicely into a backpack. I spot Dalton on my way into the terminal, and damn if that idiot isn't sitting on a big ass piece of luggage with wheels on the bottom, riding the damned thing into the airport.

"I like your new ride, little D," I yell at him. "You decide to bring that leaky-ass knucklehead engine of yours on vacation to try to replace the seals finally?"

"Hey, Abe, you're alive!" Dalton yells. "I was sure you were going to miss the flight after the night you had," Dalton waves at me cheerfully as he kicks his new ride along the sidewalk towards me. "Ha-ha, *knucklehead*. For your information, some of us need more than one pair of underwear and our teddy bear for an event like this."

"I didn't pack any underwear," I tell him solemnly, sending him into a cackling fit.

"Hey, man, if you can go commando in the Vegas heat, more power to you. You probably tuck that hog leg into your socks anyway, so it won't sweat too much."

As I turn to go inside, Dalton's cackles grow louder. I just grit my teeth and keep going, knowing full well what he saw that got him so tickled. It wouldn't fit all the way into my pack, so peeking out of the top is the head of what is obviously a rather large stuffed bear.

Thankfully, we get separated once we're inside, as his trusty steed is too big for a carry-on. While he's checking in his bag, I get through security and head on down to the boarding area. By the time I get there, they are already letting my brothers on the plane.

One of our prospects, Maddox, runs up to me as I near the lady checking our boarding passes. "Thank God," he mutters, "Chase told me not to set foot on the plane until I rounded up you and Dalton. You haven't seen him, have you, Abe?"

"He's here," I grunt. "He was still getting through security when

I got clear, but he'll be along in a few. Don't worry, you aren't going to miss the trip."

Maddox gives a relieved sigh, then wisely gets out of my way. Once the tiny ticket agent checks my credentials, I duck my head a little and head down the tunnel to the plane. The captain and his co-pilot give me the stink-eye when they come into view, but at least they greet me civilly as I wedge myself past them.

My seat, or seats I should say, are right behind Chase, Sasha, and Mercy, who are sitting in an aisle together. Chase had the decency to purchase the middle and window seat for me, so no one had to suffer the indignity of me sitting in their lap for the flight.

Mercy is talking on her phone, and she looks up at me nervously as my shadow falls over them. I smile at her and almost lean down to whisper an apology to her, but she begins to blush before she says into the phone, "Yes, I know it's the city of sin, but I'm sure I'll be fine, mother. I'm sorry I'll miss church tomorrow, but the trip is just for a few days. I'll be there next Sunday. I promise I'll call you every day, okay? Love you too. Bye." She ends the call in a rush as I shrug off my backpack.

Reaching into the overhead compartment to stow my pack, I immediately recognize the neon green bag that I remember seeing in Mercy's bedroom. Quickly, I pull the bear I bought on the way here this morning out of my pack and wedge it into her carry-on.

Slamming the compartment shut, I take my seat behind Chase and the women, and then lean up to see what they're watching on Sasha's phone.

"This is the guy covering me this week while we're out in Vegas," Sasha says, referring to a reporter on her screen. I recognize the scene he seems to be reporting from and strain to listen to the newscast.

"...live from the scene of what used to the 'Ace of Spades' pool hall here off of Old Birch Road. As we reported several weeks ago, a fire broke out here shortly after the business closed one Saturday night, leaving one man dead. Investigators today confirmed the identity of the victim as 43-year-old Johnny Martin, the owner of the facility. We were able to speak to the forensics team earlier today, at which time they confirmed the cause of the explosion and fire seems to have been a mobile methamphetamine lab, which had been parked behind the business. Police indicated that no foul play is suspected in this incident, and it appears to have been a tragic accident, proving once again the need for more drug enforcement in our area..."

Turning down the volume, Sasha looks over at Chase and asks, "Well, what do you think?"

Chase strokes his beard and tells her, "I think making meth seems pretty damned dangerous."

"No, I mean about the reporter. You don't think he's going to take my job, do you?"

Chase chuckles at that. "Not a chance, baby. Dude sounds like he sucks helium in his spare time, and he seemed nervous on camera. I think you'll be safe for a few weeks."

Sasha turns her attention to Mercy, who I swear seems to be avoiding my gaze. I lean back in my seat and start fumbling with the lap belt when Chase looks over the seat to talk to me. "You see that report about old Johnny Martin that Sasha was just showing me?" he asks, choosing his words carefully.

"Yeah," I drawl, phrasing my reply just as cautiously. "Damn shame for a man to die in an *accident* like that."

"We'll pour one out for him when we get to Vegas, yeah?" Chase says with a wink, before turning back around in his seat.

It's good to know that business, at least, was settled. I look around the cabin and wave to Chase and Torin's parents, and then give a nod to each of my brothers as Dalton and Maddox finally board. The only two people up here I didn't recognize right off are a man and woman, who I'm assuming must be Sasha's mom and dad. They're in the very back and don't look all that comfortable even with all the extra leg room. I chuckle at their expressions, right up until Dalton plops his goofy ass down in the aisle seat beside me.

With a huge grin, Dalton starts to say something, but I just hold up a hand to him and look out the window. I don't want to listen to him prattle on for hours about whatever silly-ass thoughts come into his head. I want to think about Mercy and how she'll react to the little apology gift I left her. I need to think about what else I can do to get her to forgive my outburst and what I should do to make sure that this gorgeous woman doesn't give her heart to some other man on that damned reality show.

...

Mercy

THE FLIGHT to Vegas seemed so much longer than five hours with Abe sitting just behind me. There was a palpable tension in the air and a feeling of eyes on me that made it impossible to relax on the plane. I couldn't get out of my own head long enough to just unwind with Sasha and enjoy her company knowing that, when the gentle giant boarded the plane, he had wanted to say something. After talking to Sasha and hearing what his life had been like, I feel like I understand so much more about him and why he seems to run so hot and cold. None of that, however, helps me figure out how to deal with the feelings I've developed for him or the resentment and hostility he has towards the requirements for the show.

When I finally make it to my hotel room that evening in the *Hard Rock Casino* where all of the MC and their guests are staying, I immediately drop my luggage and flop onto the bed in relief. Here, at least, I can get some privacy and get myself focused on my best friend's wedding. After lounging around for a few minutes, enjoying the silence, I call and let my mother know I arrived safely, and then grab my luggage to head into the bathroom to start unpacking.

When I set the carry-on bag on the vanity and unzip it, a big, smiling, furry, brown head immediately pops up, startling me so badly I gasp. My first panicked thought is that somehow, someway, this stalker nightmare has managed to follow me all the way to Vegas. When I carefully open the bag the rest of the way, however, a smile spreads across my face. The bear is big and wearing a soft, black, leather jacket. Between his paws he's gripping a heart, with a message that has been carefully written in bold, black permanent marker:

"FROM ABE, NOT STALKER"

I pick it up and clutch it to me. It smells like Abe, and his clothes, presumably from the time spent riding in his bag. I take it back to my bed and prop it between my pillows; then get to work around my room setting out my things. As soon as he and I have some quiet time, I plan to bring him in here and have a long, civilized discussion with him about what he and I want to do moving forward. For now, however, I've got to get ready for dinner with Sasha and her family tonight, and then tomorrow morning we've got a ton to do to get ready for the wedding.

Once I've gotten myself cleaned up and dressed, I text Sasha, who says that she and her parents are already downstairs in the casino. I let her know I'm ready and take the elevator down, so we can all grab something to eat before heading over to take a look at the venue. I'm pretty sure we're gonna try to squeeze in some salon time too.

Right when I step off the elevator, I spot Abe on the far side of the lobby. And when he turns my way, I wave at him before forming a heart with my hands while mouthing 'thank you' to him. His face breaks into a huge grin, and I'm pretty sure he even blushes under his beard. I start to push through the crowd in the lobby towards him when Sasha intercepts me.

"There you are, girl. You look great! Come on, my parents are right out front. We'll go for a little walk and check out the restaurants until we figure out what we want," Sasha says.

I start to protest as she takes me by the elbow to lead me to the door, but Sasha is pulled up short when Abe suddenly takes my other arm.

"Sorry," he rumbles, immediately letting me go.

"Oh, hi, Abe!" Sasha says. "Are you going to take care of Chase for me today?"

"Always," he tells her with a wink, before looking at me, still red-faced. I notice the crowds are still parting around him and can't help but smile at the thought of him bulling through everyone to get to me so quickly.

"Thank you for the gift," I tell Abe again.

"It was silly," he replies, lowering his eyes. "But I've never bought a woman anything and didn't know..."

"It was perfect," I tell him. "I've got to get going, but I want to talk to you. Tomorrow's going to be crazy, but you know where my room is, right?" When he nods, I continue. "Come on over tonight, and we can have some time together, okay?"

"I'll be there, Mercy. Anytime, anywhere you say," Abe tells me, giving my hand a squeeze before stepping back. "You ladies have a great time. I'll see you soon."

I finally let Sasha drag me outside as I give Abe a wave, then try to put him out of my mind as much as possible to focus on having fun with my friend. The Vegas heat hits both of us like a fist as we step outside the casino, and we rush off to rescue her parents before they melt.

CHAPTER TWENTY-TWO

Abe

I'm walking on clouds as I head back upstairs after seeing Mercy and talking to her briefly in the casino. I don't know if all is forgiven for my outburst, but I'm starting to think that, if I put myself out there, maybe we might have some sort of a chance. I had only gone down to the lobby to find some bottles of water to keep in my room. Once I go back to drop those off, I head over to the huge suite that Chase is staying in with Sasha. The rest of my brothers have already gathered there when I arrive, most of them seated at a long dining room table over by the floor-to-ceiling windows overlooking the Vegas strip.

I take a seat by Chase mid-way down the table, then Torin is the only one left standing. He's stomping around and fidgeting like a kid who has had too much candy.

He's practically bouncing off the walls, ready to find Hector's daughter right this very second.

"For the last time, we're not going to hurt her," Chase says to

Torin as I get settled down, leading me to believe that this has been an ongoing discussion.

"She's just as responsible for fucking me over as Hector is," Torin declares, but then snaps his mouth closed before explaining how. I don't think I'm the only one in the room who is clueless about what the hell those two did to Torin.

"Even so," Chase says. "She's only twenty fucking years old! We can't go around hurting women who are practically still children. That's not what we do. Am I right?" he turns and asks the group of us who made the trip. We all nod in agreement. Unless the bitch cut off Torin's cock, then I don't see any reason why he wants to physically harm her.

"That's what I thought," Chase mutters.

"She's the only way for us to draw Hector out," Torin grits out through his clenched teeth.

"Fine. We can use the rental van to take her, by force if necessary, but no one is going to hurt her more than is required to ensure her cooperation. Once Hector sets the meet, then we kill him, and the girl goes free."

"That's letting her off way too fucking easy," Torin huffs before he finally lowers himself into the chair at the head of the table and crosses his arms over his chest. The entire room goes silent. I'm not sure if anyone even considers breathing.

"What?" Torin asks with his forehead creased when he glances around and sees we've all gone still. He probably doesn't even realize that he sat down at the head of the table. Maybe it wasn't even a conscious thought. But other chairs were available, and he took that particular one. It's the first time he's sat at the head of the Savage Kings since Kennedy was killed, so I'm sure I'm not the only one who is glad to see him ready to lead again.

"Nothing," Chase says. Clearing his throat, he tells us, "After the wedding, we'll do some recon and figure out a plan to seize the girl. Grabbing her from the club she works at may be the best plan..."

"No," Torin says with a shake of his head. "This doesn't have to be an MC deal. Just me, War and Cooper can handle it. Probably less conspicuous with only the three of us."

"Are you sure?" Chase asks, looking to the two other men. They nod their agreement that they'll keep Torin out of trouble.

"We'll get her and bring her to a hotel outside of town so Hector can't find us. I'll have Reece close the bar and keep the clubhouse clear until it's all over," Torin explains.

"That's probably smart," Chase agrees with a nod.

"And you can go enjoy your honeymoon with Sasha," Torin tells him. "That shit is more important."

"I'll keep an eye on Chase and Sasha," I speak up and say. "Not in the creepy way. None of us need to be traveling alone until the score with Hector is settled."

"True," Torin agrees.

"I'll stick around in Vegas too," Sax says.

"Me too. I never want to leave this place," Dalton announces.

Chase looks to War and Cooper again, who nod their agreement with the plan.

Turning to Sax, Torin says, "Make yourself useful and call Reece. Tell him I want a rental property secured out in the country back home. Have him use one of his fake identities and go through a realtor to get it, I want a place with a code lock on the door so we don't have to be seen getting keys. Have him call me with the address when it's ready." Turning back to the table, he says, "Okay. We'll split up after the wedding. Once I have what I need from her, we'll only hold her until we can deal with Hector. If I run into any problems, I'll contact Reece with orders, and he'll get through to you guys. If any of you need me, you get messages through Reece. He'll be able to track down any of us if we have to toss our prepaids. In the meantime, Chase, congratulations, my brother. This thing with you and Sasha, it's a ray of light in the darkest time of my life. Thank you, all of you, for helping me see this through."

Everyone gives a cheer for Chase, clapping him on the back and hugging him. I give him a hug as well, but the whole time, I keep my eyes on Torin. Even after our president's little speech, and his presence at the head of the table, I have a bad feeling. I can't help but worry that, as far off the deep end as Torin is, this shit could easily go sideways.

I open my mouth to express my doubts to Chase, but what comes out instead is, "So, all the arrangements are made for the wedding out in the park?"

Chase raises an eyebrow at me, knowing that I started to ask something else. "Of course, bro. You know we had the chaplain arranged and everything else set up days ago. Something else on your mind?"

"Nah, Chase, just wanted to see what you're planning for tonight's activities. Mercy mentioned that she wanted to talk, and I was going to see if I could get free a little early since you'll have everyone else with you..."

Cracking a huge grin, Chase gathers me back into a hug and slaps me on the back. "Of course, man, absolutely. Get back here to the hotel after we eat dinner. You can skip the rest of the festivities. Sounds like you've got a much better show to make it to tonight. Just make sure you're ready for the big day?"

"I wouldn't miss this for the world. You know, when we met in prison, I never thought you'd end up being my best friend. It's a real honor to be here with you and Sasha. Seeing you guys so happy together has been...well, it's been kind of inspirational for me. I never knew love like this existed. I hope I can find something like it one day."

"Damn, Abe, Mercy has done a number on you," Chase says, chuckling for a moment, before looking at me seriously. "I hate to say it, brother, but I think she might be the first truly good woman you have ever known. I can't imagine what it's been like trying to wrap your head around that after what you've been through. If you need to talk about anything, you let me know. For now, though, let's break into that fridge and start making a dent in all that beer I brought!"

I do as he asks and crack open the refrigerator to find it almost overflowing with different brands of beer. Lined up on the counter are two-liter soda bottles and all sorts of brands of whiskey, vodka, and tequila. Someone cranks up the stereo, and I start pouring drinks for my brothers, but I can never quite get into the party. For one, my guts are in a knot wondering how things are going to go with Mercy tonight. What worries me even more, though, is the haunted expression I see on Torin's face when he's sitting by himself. If there's such a thing as resting maniac face, Chase's older brother has it.

CHAPTER TWENTY-THREE

Mercy

THE AFTERNOON AND NIGHT PASSES IN A HEAT-STRICKEN BLUR. Sasha, her parents, and I drive all over the city, checking out the park where the wedding will be held, confirming the catering and other arrangements, and then get made over at the salon. By the time we get done with the late dinner and show that Sasha booked for us, I've had way too much to drink for one night, so I tell the girls goodbye and take the elevator back up to my room. Or maybe it will be *our* room, I remind myself, since Abe should be coming up as soon as the guys are finished with their bachelor night out.

Pulling my keycard from my purse, it takes me two tries to get the damn lights to go green so that I can pull on the handle and stagger inside.

Something crunches under my heel as the door shuts. I look down and find a piece of paper someone must have slid under the door. Figuring it's a room service invoice or maybe even a sweet note from Abe, I pick it up and open it.

My dearest Mercy,

I warned you to stop with the unladylike behavior that is an embarrassment to yourself and to me, your future husband. You didn't listen, and now I'm incredibly angry and hurt. You should be glad that I love you so much or I may not be able to forgive you for spending every night with that big buffoon biker. He's not the man for you, and we both know it.

Your One True Love.

Oh, my god! He's here, in the hotel! Who the hell is this lunatic? Did he follow me here? How the hell did he know where I was going?

I need to find Abe right fucking now. Pulling out my phone from my purse, I try to call him; but there's no freaking signal in the room. Rather than stay in this room alone for another second, I peer out the peephole to make sure the hall is clear before I open the door and run to the elevator with my purse and the letter. I think I drop my keycard somewhere in the commotion, but that's the last thing on my mind. I can get another one.

When I'm safely on the elevator, I try to call Abe again; but it still says no service. Damn it!

In the lobby, I walk up to the check-in counter and tell the first clerk I see, "There's someone stalking me, and he's here in the casino."

"Oh, wow," the woman replies, eyes widening in worry. I'm glad to see that she's at least taking this seriously. "I'll call security," she says when she picks up the phone.

"Thank you," I reply on an exhale as I try to reach Abe again. It finally starts ringing this time. He picks up immediately.

"Hey, Red. I'm on my way to your room," he says.

"Abe! Thank god I got you," I say in a rush. "He's here. He's been in the hotel and left a note in my room."

"Are you fucking kidding me!" he exclaims. "Where are you?"

"I'm in the lobby at the check-in counter," I tell him.

"Stay there!" he orders. "I'm on my way down!"

"Okay—" I start to say; but as my eyes sweep around the busy casino, they land on a familiar looking dumpy man with shaggy, brown hair. I've seen him before, I'm certain, but it takes me a minute to figure out where. Seeing my gaze on him, he smiles broadly and then waves a hand at me before he starts walking toward me.

When he's only five feet away it hits me.

Joseph.

That's it! I've seen him most Sundays at my mother's church. She's tried to set me up with him for years. I was polite to him, but he definitely gave off a creepy vibe. What is he doing in Vegas the same weekend that I'm here? He's in khakis and a short-sleeve button-down, like he's dressed for church. Seems odd that a Bible thumper like him would be here in sin city. It'd be like seeing my mother...

Hold on a second.

Joseph couldn't be the person following me, could he?

Only a few people knew I was coming – Ryan, the show's producer, and my mother.

Has Joseph been chatting up my mother to keep tabs on me?

"Mercy," he says as he draws near me, his pale blue eyes sparkling. "It's always such a pleasure to see you in person." His left hand is buried in his khaki pocket, but he raises his right one to reach for me, before I quickly draw back a step.

"Joseph," I say sternly, my eyes darting around and spotting Abe pushing his way through the crowded lobby. "What brings you out to Vegas this week?"

"You, my love," he says, his eyes narrowing as he follows my gaze and sees the huge, bearded figure drawing near us. "I had hoped that you would come to your senses and realize I cannot allow this man to be a part of your life any longer, but I suppose your female mind requires a display of dominance from me to prove my feelings."

"Mercy!" Abe roars as he storms over to us. "Who the hell is this guy?"

"Abe, be careful. I think it's him!" I scream as Joseph finally draws his left hand out of his pocket, some sort of small tube wrapped in his fist.

Abe sees it as well and jerks his head up just as Joseph points it at his face and unleashes a torrent of thick red liquid that soaks Abe's beard and t-shirt. "Take that, you..." Joseph screeches, just before Abe whips his arm around, smashing the smaller man's jaw with an audible crack.

Joseph drops to the floor instantly, the can of pepper spray he had been palming falling to the ground beside him. Abe lets out an explosive breath of air, blinking down at Joseph for just a moment before bending down to snatch up the can. The desk clerk I spoke to moments ago has run across the lobby and is thankfully sprinting back towards us with two men in 'security' shirts following her.

Before they can get close to us, Abe shoves the pepper spray into Joseph's face and, still roaring, empties the rest of the can into his eyes and mouth. Abe gets back to his feet just as one of the security guards rushes over and grabs his arm, while Joseph rolls and screeches on the ground at their feet.

I grab the shirt of the security officer, who is trying vainly to get a hold on Abe. "Not him! He's...he's my boyfriend! It's that guy on the ground who's been stalking me!" I tell him.

"Wait," the guard says, dropping his hands from Abe. "*This guy* is your boyfriend?" he asks incredulously, staring up at Abe.

"Yes! That man on the ground, his name is Joseph. He...he goes to church with my mother, and he's been stalking me for weeks! We're from North Carolina, and the police have been following me trying to catch him, and..." Abe lays a hand on me, instantly calming me as I realize I was rambling.

"Hold that guy and get the police. Maybe an ambulance, too," Abe instructs the guards.

"Are you all right, big fella?" the other guard asks from where he now has Joseph on his belly while he kneels on his back.

"Shit burns a bit," Abe acknowledges, as he begins to gingerly take off his shirt in the lobby, trying to make sure that none of the spray touches him. "Dumbass mostly just hosed down my beard and neck. I think I should be able to wash it off."

"Can you two hold him until the police arrive?" I ask the guards, who nod in acknowledgement. "I'm going to take my boyfriend up to our room and try to help him clean up." Then, I turn to the desk clerk, who is now back behind the counter. "My name is Mercy Daniels. Can you pull up my room number and issue me a new key quickly?" I ask her.

"Of course," she confirms, typing at her terminal. "With this situation, we would definitely want to reset your key cards and issue you new ones. I'll stay here and let the police know what room they can find you in once they review security footage and deal with this person. I'll send them up to get your statement. Here you go, ma'am," she says as she slides me a new card.

"Thank you so much, for everything," I tell her. "Abe, come on, let's try to clean you up," I say to him as I grab his hand and lead him towards the elevators. He's making a brave show in front of the crowd that's gawking at us in the lobby. But from his squinted eyes and shallow breathing, I can tell that he is in a lot more pain than he's letting on.

"Thanks, Red," he whispers as the elevator doors close on just the two of us.

"Don't thank me. He could've had a gun or...or a knife, or...oh god, Abe, he could have killed you!" I realize in horror.

"I've dealt with worse shit than him. Hell, I got shot a few weeks ago," he says with a feeble grin while rubbing his chest where the enormous bruise is starting to heal and holding his ruined t-shirt away from his body.

I knew it was more than just a bar fight! He must have been shot through a bulletproof vest. What if he hadn't been wearing one? Jeez! When I frown at Abe in concern, he winks at me and says, "I don't care if he had pulled a grenade out. You know I would have jumped on it for you. I'd do any fucking thing for you. Shit, listen to me. I sound like that Joseph freak."

"No, you don't," I tell him, looking up to stare in his dark eyes.

"Abe, I..." I get interrupted as the elevator dings for our floor, and I lead him out by his hand without finishing.

Using the new keycard, I open my door; and Abe leaves his t-shirt in a smelly heap in the hallway. Once I've got him inside, I slap the security bolt across the door as Abe immediately heads for the bathroom. When I follow him inside, he's running the sink full blast, scrubbing furiously at his neck and chest.

"Whew!" he says, looking at me bleary-eyed in the mirror. "Water helps a little, I guess, but this stuff is nasty! It didn't get in my nose or eyes, thank god, but...damn, Red, do you think I'm gonna have to shave off my beard?"

"Oh, Abe, no!" I protest, knowing how much he would hate that right before the wedding and all the pictures. "Hold on a second. Let me...let me look it up online." Pulling out my phone, I search the internet, trying to figure out how to treat skin exposed to pepper spray.

"Damn, that's handy, Red," Abe comments, still scrubbing at his face. "I always have to use old school prepaid phones with the club. Having internet access must be nice."

I scan the page I find briefly, then rush over to my vanity, looking for a small bottle I keep in my bag. "Okay, it says that one thing we can try is baby oil. Hold still," I order him as I turn him towards me, taking one of the hotel towels to wring out his beard and mop at his chest.

Using a fresh towel, so I don't just smear the foul-smelling spray still clinging to him, I dump the small bottle of baby oil across his chest, and then begin rubbing it across his neck. I use the towel to wring out his beard with the oil, then work my way back down to his chest.

"I don't know what that maniac was thinking, confronting me in such a public place," I tell Abe, just to break the awkward silence between us. "I mean, he could've been preparing to kidnap me, or... but you were there. You've been there for me through all of this. Thank you, so much, Abe."

Unconsciously, while I was talking, my hands had strayed down to Abe's rock hard and sculpted abdomen, where the baby oil had run in channels down across his muscular form. My free hand was rubbing the oil across his stomach; and when I realize what I'm doing, I look down to see the outline of Abe's cock straining mightily against the fabric of his jeans. My breath catches in my throat as my mouth waters remembering how I sucked that glorious cock the other night, and I clear my throat when I joke, "So...you seem to be feeling better."

I start to step back, but Abe catches my hand, sliding it through the oil on his abs, all the way down to the button on his jeans. "It still hurts a bit...down there," he says, smiling at me.

I grin back up at him and drop the towel I was wiping him with into the sink. I quickly pop the button on his jeans and sink to my knees on the bathroom rug, shimmying his jeans down his thick, muscular thighs until his cock bobs free, almost smacking me on my chin. I grab his shaft with my right hand, guiding him into my mouth while my still oily left hand cups his balls.

"Fuck, Red, your mouth is amazing," Abe moans as my mouth glides down his cock. When his head hits the back of my throat, I swallow fiercely, and then force even more of him down my throat. "Christ, oh, Mercy. *Mercy*..." Abe chants as he disappears into my mouth. "No one's ever managed to do that, Red," he gasps.

My eyes are watering when I come back up for air, letting all but the head of his shaft go free. My left hand keeps working his sack as I shorten my strokes, only taking half of Abe at a time. As my pace quickens, Abe grabs my hair, making me think he is about to come. Instead, he pulls me back gently and then guides me to my feet.

"You're not feeling better yet, are you?" I ask him playfully. His only reply is to jerk the thin straps of my light summer dress down my arms, then force it down my hips until it puddles around my feet. Standing there in only my bra and heels, Abe gazes down my body, lust and adoration in his eyes.

"Still no panties, Red?" Abe grins. "That's my girl. Turn around," he orders.

I turn to face the bathroom mirror and grip the edge of the sink as Abe moves behind me. The expression of pain is gone from his face, and I watch his oiled torso gleaming in the lights as he places one hand on my hip while lining himself up with my slick entrance. With one smooth, slow stroke, he buries himself deep inside of me.

"*OHMYFUCKINGGOD!*" I scream as he reaches around to grab my breasts, standing me up and pressing my back into his slick chest. This angle is even better, so deep inside me I can barely breathe. He begins rocking gently against me, one hand cupping my breast as the other trails down my belly to find my clit.

"Jesus, Mercy. No one's ever made me feel like this," Abe whispers to me as his hand strokes through my soft, red curls, rubbing my most sensitive area while continuing his slow grind.

"No one's ever made me feel," I tell him, turning my head towards him when he catches my mouth in a kiss. With a hot, clenching rush, my lower belly tightens, and I come explosively as Abe buries himself inside me. "Oh, god, Abe. No one's ever...no one's ever...made me feel like this!" I cry.

The orgasm seems to rock me for minutes as Abe continues his slow, gentle motions behind me. Once the echoes of it begin to fade, I almost fall forward, but Abe catches me as he gently pulls his thick cock free of me. "No, not yet," I whisper, looking back at him in longing.

"Shhh, not yet, Mercy," Abe reassures me as he turns me around to face him. Reaching down to cup my bottom in both of his huge hands, he picks me up and clutches me to his chest as my legs wrap around him. Rather than impaling me on his still throbbing cock, he walks with me back into the bedroom, throwing the sheets back on the bed with one hand before slowly laying me down, then kissing his way up my belly and breasts until we're face to face.

"I want to see it in your eyes when you come for me," he says, pushing my hair back until it's spread out on the bed behind me. "I want to take you slow. I want to show you..." he trails off as he shifts his hips, once again guiding his thick cock into my body.

"I want to see you, too, Abe," I tell him, reaching around to grab his shoulders and wrapping my legs around his upper thighs. As I pull him deeper inside me, whatever else we wanted to say to each other is lost in our passion. Abe's lips crash down onto mine, his oily beard tickling me all the way down between my breasts as we make love.

All sense of time is lost to me as Abe rocks above me, his groans and my cries of pleasure passing between us. By the time I feel Abe's thrusts begin to quicken, the bed is a ruin of sweaty sheets, and I've lost track of how many times he's gazed into my eyes as I come apart for him. I tighten my grip on his legs and shoulders as he hammers into me, forcing him to meet my gaze as he takes a huge breath, and then I feel his orgasm explode into me, the hot rush sending me over the edge into a final, screaming frenzy of my own.

Abe collapses onto his elbows, holding his weight above me so he doesn't suffocate me while he recovers. After a few silent minutes where the two of us simply stroke each other's bodies and kiss, he finally withdraws his swollen cock, leaving a gaping emptiness inside me.

"Damn, Red, I think that was the best we've done together so far," Abe says, smiling down at me as he stands by the bed.

"I know it was," I assure him. "Every time I'm with you I think it's the best sex of my life, but then you go and up your game again."

"I've gotta hit the shower and wash all this off," Abe says, pointing at his still oily chest and stomach. "Do you want to join me?" he offers.

"Definitely," I reply. "Go get it started while I lie here a bit longer. I don't think my legs will hold me just yet."

I give him a few minutes to get the shower ready and clean up; and then, with trembling steps, I follow him into the bathroom. As I slide the glass shower door to the side and step inside, Abe is enough of a gentleman to move aside and let me get to the hot water. Once

I've had a chance to soap up and rinse off, he joins me under the spray, and our lips find each other again. Only a few moments later, I gasp in surprise as I feel his cock bob up between us, pulsing again and demanding attention.

"Abe, that's got to be physically impossible," I say with a laugh as I break our kiss.

"Nothing's impossible with you," he replies. "You up for it, though? It's okay if you need to tap out. I'd understand."

Instead of dignifying that silliness with a response, I simply turn around and brace my palms against the wall of the shower stall and then shake my ass at him invitingly as I grin over my shoulder. Abe just smiles back at me as he adjusts the shower head to make sure we both stay warm before lining himself up with my still slick entrance.

Making gentle, sweet love with Abe was mind-blowing, but so is the brutal, steamy pounding he gives me as we're locked together in the shower. All rational thought is lost as Abe ravages me, only his strong hands and his iron cock holding me steady as my legs finally turn to wet noodles from the constant orgasm assault. When I finally feel Abe reach his own shuddering climax, he gently washes us both down one more time, before shutting off the water and wrapping me in a towel.

While we're both catching our breath and drying off in the bathroom after our shower, I hear a knock on the door to my room.

"Miss Daniels? This is the Las Vegas City Police," calls a man from outside.

"Crap," I mutter before I pull away from Abe. I grab my bathrobe from the hook behind the door, then wink at him as I walk out and pull the bathroom door partially closed. "I'll talk to them and give my statement. You find your pants," I order him.

"I'll be right out if you need anything," he agrees.

Going to the hotel door, I check the peephole to see that it is indeed the police. There are two officers, one male and one female. Unlocking the door, I open it and greet them with a huge smile. "I'm so glad to see you, officers. Did you have any trouble taking him into custody?"

"No, ma'am, no trouble at all," the female officer says. "I'm Officer Price, and this is Officer Ramos." She makes introductions as they step inside. "We just need to get your statement as to what happened leading up to the events down in the lobby. The suspect, Mr. Joseph Stanly, is in custody and is currently being transported to a local hospital for treatment of his injuries. We're waiting to hear back from North Carolina about his criminal record."

"You guys, um, keep an officer on him, don't you?" I ask nervously.

"Oh, yes, ma'am, absolutely," Officer Ramos reassures me. "We don't take chances with people like him. Your boyfriend, or body-guard, whoever that fellow was, though, he did a number on Mr. Stanly. His jaw appears to be broken, and the pepper spray...well, I know from experience that a face full of that stuff will leave you in agony for quite some time."

"We were lucky," I tell the officers. "Abe, my...friend, he mostly just got sprayed in his beard. We've been trying to wash it out," I tell them lamely, knowing how I look, flushed and disheveled in my bathrobe, and knowing that the room probably smells like an orgy.

"Well, ma'am, we won't take up much of your time. If you could just answer a few questions for us..." As Officer Price begins going through a list of what seem like form questions, I catch a glimpse of Abe smiling at me from the bathroom. Returning his grin, I do my best to guide the officers through everything that has transpired in the last few weeks, until they finally seem to have all of the details that they need.

"All right, Ms. Daniels," Officer Ramos finally says. "I think we have everything. We'll be in touch with you soon to keep you apprised of the charges that will be filed and upcoming court appear-ances. For now, please relax and enjoy the rest of your stay out here. We'll make sure that Mr. Stanly, at least, doesn't cause you any more trouble."

Once I show the pair of officers out the door, Abe finally emerges from the bathroom. "Didn't mean to be a creeper through all that," he says. "But it looked like you were fine, and I don't much like talking to cops."

"Ugh, tell me about it. I'm exhausted," I reply. I shed the bathrobe, dropping it onto a chair by the bed. The sheets seem to be dry for the most part, so I put them back into some semblance of order; then stand up straight with a hand on my hip to look at Abe. "You coming to bed, big man?" I ask him.

"Mercy, I...I," Abe swallows hard, and I see a look of sadness in his eyes before he continues. "I can't stay all night. I'll have to get to my stuff early tomorrow and get cleaned up for the wedding."

"Ugh, don't remind me about the early start," I joke, wondering what's really on his mind. "If you need to sneak out early, I understand. For now, though...well, today has been insane. Take off your pants and hold me, Abe. I need you."

Abe just smiles and nods. I climb into bed and snuggle down into the sheets, leaving room for him to join me. Whatever is on his mind we can work out together in the coming days, after the wedding. For now, as I burrow up against his side, smelling our scents mixed together, everything is right with my world.

CHAPTER TWENTY-FOUR

Abe

I WANT NOTHING MORE THAN TO FALL ASLEEP WITH MERCY IN my arms, but Chase has made some special arrangements for his wedding. It's going to be an outdoor ceremony at Sunset Park, and it starts at eight o' clock in the morning. The heat out here is oppressive, so he and Sasha decided to do their vows early, take all their photos, then retire to the casino for a big reception. I'm one of Chase's groomsmen so I have to be ready before daybreak to go out and help get everything set up with the rest of my brothers.

So, after we make love one more time in bed and Mercy drifts off to sleep, I gently tuck her in and find my boots and pants to reluctantly sneak out. I know how well I sleep when I'm in this woman's arms, and Mercy was a little worried she might miss her alarm, too, if she stays wrapped up with me.

Once I'm back in my room, I call downstairs to set up a wake-up call in case my old phone doesn't do it for me; then take care of getting my suit laid out and do some ironing. Mercy offered to help me with it when I told her I was worried it was going to take me hours, but I assured her I could *probably* do it myself without burning the hotel down.

As soon as that's done, I take care of trimming my beard and washing it again. All of the pepper spray residue is gone, but the oil we used to get it off made it clumpy. If any of my brothers saw me grooming myself like this to get ready, I'd be the laughing stock of the MC; but I'm not about to mess up my best friend's wedding by showing up looking homeless.

Once I'm satisfied that all I need is water and a comb to get myself presentable when I wake up, I finally lie down to get some quick shut-eye. My head has barely dented the pillow when the damned phone starts ringing, and it takes me almost a full minute to figure out it's not my cell but the room phone. When I pick it up and hear the robocall announce the time, I spring up, wide-awake and ready for the big day. Hell, if I'm excited, I can only imagine how Chase and Sasha are feeling right about now.

I get a quick shower, suit up, and then I head downstairs to meet my brothers in the rental van. Dalton, Maddox, Sax, Cooper and War have already gotten all the gear we rented loaded up, so I hop in the back to wait for Torin and Chase. And before the sun peeks over the horizon, we're at the park getting everything arranged.

The area that Sasha had picked out is a huge, open air, picnic setting covered entirely by a giant white umbrella shaped canvas. The grounds were kept in pristine condition, so when we pile out of the van, we get straight to work on the decorations. We have hundreds of yards of white silk flowers to string around, along with dozens of more conventional floral arrangements that arrive as the sun began to rise.

The caterer arrives at about six-thirty to set up a breakfast spread for everyone as well as something they called a mimosa bar. I'm not much on champagne, but the juice is welcome even in the relatively cool morning light. By the time we have the gazebo and podium all set up and the chairs arranged, the guests start to arrive.

Sasha has her own special limo to bring her to the park when it's time. Chase is busy entertaining the guests spread around the picnic tables eating, so in the final few minutes before the ceremony, I walk the grounds, just keeping an eye out for trouble. I had seen Mercy when she arrived in her long, elegant, black dress, and we had exchanged a wave, but I hadn't had a chance to talk to her yet this morning. I won't get to until the reception most likely, as she's the maid-of-honor and will be walking down the aisle with Torin, the best man. We'll have to be in a bunch of photos afterwards, so hopefully I can get close to her then.

When the small orchestra we hired gets done tuning up and begins to play something that I vaguely recognize as wedding music, I walk over to stand with Chase.

"How's everything look, man? You think she'll like it?" I ask him.

"You guys really came through for us out here, Abe. It looks damned good," Chase replies as he glances around the scene. "I heard you had some excitement last night. You doing all right today?"

"Yeah, brother. Mercy and I finally got that dude that was stalking her nailed down. Crazy bastard goes to her mother's church and followed her out here. He tried to confront her down in the lobby last night."

"He didn't hurt her, did he?" Chase asks, his face alarmed.

"Nah, man, nothing like that. He never got to lay a hand on her. She called me, and I ran in on him, busted him up some. He was a chubby, little prick, but he could have been real dangerous for her."

"War said he heard you got hit with mace or something," Chase said.

"Pepper spray, yeah. Dumbass shot me in the beard with it."

Chase starts laughing, drawing everyone's eyes over to us. "Oh, god, man, I would have paid to have been there when he hosed you down and realized that rug on your face was armor. I bet his expression was priceless."

"I don't think he even had a chance to realize it didn't work on me," I grin. "I put him on his ass before he could figure out what was going on. After that, I got Mercy out of there, and..."

"Ah, man, hear that?" Chase interrupts me. "That song's my cue. I have to go up with the chaplain. Take your places everyone!" Chase calls as he walks away.

Mercy is at the end of the aisle with Torin, who looks decidedly uncomfortable in his tuxedo standing next to my fiery red-headed angel. She flashes me a grin as I walk past them, down towards the gazebo where Chase had asked me to stand, and Torin gives me a single grave nod.

When we're all in position, the orchestra strikes up the bridal procession, and Torin walks arm in arm with Mercy down to join us. He goes over and stands next to Chase, while I stay a little off to the side.

A moment later, all eyes are drawn to the back as Sasha makes her appearance. She's radiant in the early morning light, glowing in a sleeveless ivory gown with a short train trailing behind her. The bouquet of white roses she holds matches the decorations we hung all around the enclosure. As she marches slowly down the aisle, she and Chase don't take their eyes off of each other. I spare a glance at Mercy standing on the other side of the gazebo and catch her glancing at me with a broad grin as her eyes sparkle with unshed tears. God help me, but in my eyes, she outshines the bride today, and I can't look away from her as the bride and groom take their places and the ceremony commences.

I don't pay much attention to the vows or the exchanging of the rings as I keep my eyes on the crowd and the spectators in the park who had gathered on the outskirts to watch the show. Chase had stationed me up here not just as his best friend, but also as a guard. A week ago, when they were finalizing the arrangements, they had gone ahead and shipped a few pistols out here to the hotel, so the package would be waiting on us. I have one of them securely strapped under my suit jacket and am vigilant throughout the ceremony.

I didn't need to worry, thank God. After Chase and Sasha seal their vows with a deep, passionate kiss, they walk back down the aisle to cheers and applause. The photographer sweeps in and starts ordering us all into positions for the wedding shoot. It takes longer than I could have ever imagined, as he drags us all over the park, looking for the perfect shot.

During what I hope is our final photo, Mercy's cell phone begins to loudly vibrate non-stop in the little clutch she's carrying.

"Excuse me, everyone," she apologizes as she walks away from the group photo. I glance over at Chase and Sasha, who both give me the nod to follow her.

Mercy doesn't notice me as I walk over to check on her.

"Now wait, Ryan. What happened? A tabloid story?" Mercy asks nervously.

I remember that Ryan was the name of the producer on her show, *Queen of Hearts*, and so I keep quiet so I won't interrupt a call that must be important.

"Pictures and a video of when the stalker attacked me? God, I hate that it's out there already. I told you I didn't want that getting publicized. He's been arrested, thankfully, so that's no longer a problem," she says, then pauses.

"Another problem?" Mercy asks after listening to Ryan for a moment. "My boyfriend? No, that's not...oh, okay," she adds, pausing again for a long time. "Yes, I can do that, sure. We can go ahead and get in front of this. I'll catch the flight and see you on set tomorrow. Uh-huh, thanks, Ryan." Mercy says, hanging up the phone and then turning to see me standing nearby.

"Abe!" she gasps. "Thank God. I need to talk to you. I've got to catch a flight back to Wilmington in a few hours so that I can finish filming the show."

"That's what the call was about?" I ask her, disappointment obvious in my voice. I had hoped...well, if I'm being honest I had secretly hoped that she would just quit the damned show.

"Someone was filming and took photos of Joseph confronting me yesterday. Apparently when I told security that you were my boyfriend, it got recorded. Ryan's worried that if it gets out there before we've got the show wrapped up, it will tank the whole production. He wants to get the final ceremony done as soon as possible so they can start airing promos," Mercy explains.

"The final ceremony where you pick the man who has 'won your heart'?" I ask, sarcasm heavy in my voice. "Why did you say that then, Mercy? Why did you tell security that I was your boyfriend and not your bodyguard?"

"It just popped out of my mouth, Abe. I didn't have a lot of time in the moment to think it over, did I?" Mercy says, matching my sarcasm and glare with her own.

"So that's it then? Your stalker is caught, and you're just gonna jet off back to your show to pick the man of your dreams?" I yell, wounded beyond words that she is going through with the stupid fucking show. I'm irrationally angry, knowing full well I never asked her to quit the damned thing, but hoped that she would make the decision on her own. "You've used me for what you needed. And now that you've gotten dirty in the gutter for a bit, you're just going to leave me behind? Women never stick around in my life, so why should you, right?"

"No, Abe," Mercy says through gritted teeth, as tears began to slide down her beautiful cheeks. "That was not what I was going to do. You're not the only one who's been heartbroken before. Don't you understand that? I've given everything to a man, and he humiliated me and threw me away. You know that, and yet here you are, expecting me to be the one to lay myself out there for you when you won't even meet me halfway. I told you I can't break this contract, because it will ruin me financially. It's just a show, an act. I was starting to think that maybe *you* had what it takes to win my heart. But the way you act, Abe, when you won't open up to me, I'm not sure that you have what it takes either."

I stand there stunned as Mercy breaks down in tears, unable to think of what to say as she starts to walk away. "Mercy, wait, don't go..." I belatedly start.

"Goodbye, Abe. Tell Sasha I'm sorry I have to leave," she sobs before lifting her long, black dress and breaking into a run for the parking lot.

I'm at a complete loss after hearing what she said. She's going to go finish the show, but she said it wasn't real. Deep down I fucking know that. I was there every damn day, and there was no chemistry between her and any of the men.

And she's right, all I've been there to do for her is fuck and fight when she needed me. I've never even offered to give her more than that or let down my guard enough for her to see the feelings I have for her. How the hell could she know that she's the greatest thing that's ever happened to me if the words never got past my lips?

While I'm still standing there staring off into the distance, Chase walks over to me, tugging at the knot of his tie in aggravation. "Mercy leaving?" he asks.

"I love her," I say out loud, to no one in particular while shoving my hand in my suit pocket to run my fingertips over the dime I've kept on me since the first day we met. Fuck, I'm pretty sure I loved Mercy from the moment I saw her.

"Yeah," Chase agrees good-naturedly. "Sasha told me."

"What?" I ask in shock, turning to face my best friend. "Did Mercy say something to her?"

"Nah, nothing like that," he replies. "She's good at spotting this sort of thing. Sasha saw how you two acted around each other. She was worried that you and Mercy are both kind of damaged, though. You know, you've got your shit with your mom, and you've never had a real relationship with a woman because you don't think you deserve it. And Mercy, well, she had that bad break-up and shit after the last reality show. Sasha thought that you both might be too hard-headed to let shit just happen and give each other a chance."

"Well why the hell didn't she tell me that?" I demand.

"She told me I should talk to you about it," Chase says with a grin. "But let's face it, I've been a little busy."

"So what the hell am I supposed to do now? I mean, how do I let her know that I...how do I let her know how I feel and shit without getting shot down, especially if she's off to go finish that fucking show?"

"Damn, Abe, didn't you learn anything from all my years of pining after Sasha? You can't just leave shit unsaid, man. You gotta speak up and put yourself out there. Yeah, you might get shot down, but maybe you won't. It's all about making the grand gesture and taking the chance. You know, the boom-box outside the window, the ridiculous, cheesy-as-fuck proclamation of love? Women need to hear it, man. You can't just take that shit for granted. If you really want her, then you've got to bust in and proclaim that shit for the world to hear. Especially with a woman like Mercy, who tried to do it herself and got burned so badly in the past. You've got to take the leap on this one if you're really serious about her. You understand what I'm saying?"

"Yeah, Chase. I never really thought about it. But with what happened with you and Sasha, with the shit that you didn't get to say, and all that happened...I know what I have to do. Grand gestures even if I look like a fool, right?"

"That's right. Now get the hell out of here."

"I can't," I tell him. "I'm supposed to have your back."

"I'll be fine. Dalton, Sax and Maddox can stick around for a little longer while War and Cooper help Torin take care of business. I can spare you for a while, man, especially for something this important."

"Are you sure?" I ask.

"Go fucking get her, Abe."

Chase didn't have to tell me twice. With a nod of determination, I take off across the parking lot, looking for a taxi to drive me back to the hotel. I briefly think about calling Mercy; but after what Chase said about grand gestures, a much better plan quickly starts to take form in my head.

It's time to go big or go home.

CHAPTER TWENTY-FIVE

Mercy

THE LAST TWENTY-FOUR HOURS WERE SUCH A WHIRLWIND THAT I'm only able to finally relax even the slightest bit when I'm inside my trailer that's outside the mansion where we'll be filming the final episode of *Queen of Hearts*. After rushing back to the *Hard Rock* in Vegas and grabbing my things, I had to hustle to the airport, try to get a little bit of sleep, and then get here to film. We've spent the day doing the final "dates" with the remaining three bachelors. And tonight, as the sun sets, we'll do the final ceremony where I'm supposed to make my choice.

As I sit at my vanity letting the hairdresser and makeup artist apply their finishing touches, my thoughts once again turn back to Abe. I haven't heard anything from him since I left him out at Sunset Park. That hard-headed mountain of a man is infuriating, and I can barely control my frustration with him! When he lets his guard down around me, he's more than I could have ever imagined in a partner. But whenever he gets overwhelmed or even hints at expressing a feeling, he retreats to his big, bad biker persona. It's a sexy as hell persona, but it's not one he needs to use to defend himself from his feelings. Especially any feelings he may have for me.

The trailer door opens from the outside, and then my brief moment of peace evaporates into thin air when I see the thin woman with big, poofy, red hair step inside the trailer.

"Mom? What the...what are you doing here?" I ask her while trying to pick my jaw up off the ground.

"Ryan asked if I wanted to come, so of course I told him yes," she replies. "Don't you need my help to pick the man you're gonna spend the rest of your life with?"

"That's...no, mother. I think I can handle this on my own."

"Oh really?" she asks while the hairdresser and makeup artist continue working on me.

"Yes. You don't exactly have the best judge of character."

She huffs and crosses her arms in front of a floral dress that she's owned since the eighties. "Why would you say that?"

"Joseph."

I'm barely able to say his name without shivering in disgust.

"Well? What about him? He's a good Christian man."

"He was a stalker, mother! A pervy, psycho, creepy stalker."

"I beg your pardon," she starts to say, but I cut her off with details.

"He stole my panties, my *worn* panties, and left me creepy notes. He was watching me from a roof in my neighborhood! And guess what. He followed me to Vegas! Did you tell him where I was?"

My mother just blinks her green eyes, which I inherited, at me.

"There must be some mistake," she finally says.

"Nope. No mistake. Joseph won't make it to church for a while. The Vegas PD locked him up when he hosed down my...my body-guard with pepper spray in the casino."

"I-I don't know what to say," she mutters, which is definitely a first for my mother. "I'm so sorry, Mercy."

"It's okay," I tell her, because I don't want her to blame herself even though it's most likely her fault that he always knew where I was.

"I probably should've told you that I lost that spare key to your cottage that you gave me," she tells me softly.

"Yeah, you probably should have," I agree with a roll of my eyes. Guess that explains how he got in without breaking windows. "Let's just forget it, okay?"

"Okay," she agrees with a sheepish nod. For once in her life, I think my mother is embarrassed. "So, are you excited about tonight?" she eventually asks, breaking the silence.

"I'm...nervous," I admit, but I don't explain why. What I plan to do could void my contract, and then I would have to pay back money that I've already spent on rent and my mother's bills.

"Oh, Mercy, I would be too! Having those three gentlemen calling on you, all determined to be the best for you...well, it's over-whelming! I'll...I'll be happy for you no matter who you decide to pick."

"You'll be happy for me no matter what? You promise?" I ask her.

"Yes."

Grinning at my mother, I tell her, "I'm gonna hold you to that. If you ever start to slip up, whether it's today or a year from now, I'll just say Joseph's name to remind you that I'm a grown woman and I'm capable of trusting my own gut. And my heart."

"Okay," she agrees with a nod right before there's a hard knock on my trailer door.

"Come in!" I call, and then Randy, the producer's assistant, cracks open the door.

"The bachelors are ready for you, Miss Daniels. Can you be down in five?" Randy asks.

"Of course, I'm ready now. Right, ladies?"

"Oh, honey, you're more than ready," Denise, my makeup artist, says while removing the apron she had tied around me to prevent any powder from falling on my dress.

"You look marvelous!" Andrea, the hairstylist, agrees.

Tonight, I'm wearing a long, sleeveless, red sequined gown, cut low in the front and tight at the hip to emphasize what Ryan had called my "queenly glory."

"You look beautiful, Mercy," my mother says when I get to my feet.

"Thanks, Mom. I'm glad you're here," I tell her before I go over and give her a hug.

After thanking Denise and Andrea again, I follow Randy out of the trailer and over to the southern garden that's decorated in a ton of white lights. That's where we'll be filming the finale at the ocean overlook. My three suitors are already gathered there in their black tuxes, sipping drinks and chatting amongst themselves. Each of them beams at me as I arrive, coming over to give me a hug, and in Zeke's case, trying to steal a kiss, which I quickly divert with my cheek before breaking away. I introduce them quickly to my mother before Ryan rushes over and guides me away from the group of men. He leads me to a podium they've set up with a heart-shaped pin as big as my palm lying on a square of black velvet.

"All right, Mercy. Thanks again for coming back so quickly so we can get ahead of this with some promos before TMZ or someone else picks up the story. Now, you know what you have to do. You'll call the first man forward who is not your choice and say a few words to him about the time you spent together. Then, when it's just the last two, we want you to hesitate a few moments before announcing your choice. We can edit it for a more dramatic pause, so don't worry about that part too much. Are you ready to make your decision?"

"I am," I confirm with a smile.

"You going to give me a hint, or are you still insisting on keeping everyone in the dark until the big moment?" he asks with a grin.

"I don't want you to lose the magic!" I tease him. "You'll have to wait just a little longer like everyone else."

"All right, everyone!" Ryan says with a broad smile. "Take your positions. We're ready to shoot this finale!" The three suitors line up in front of me, and the rest of the crew quickly takes their positions. "Let me get silence on the set, please!" Ryan calls.

Everyone pauses a moment as we all listen to a thunderous rumbling that seems to grow louder before abruptly fading away. Ryan looks around at the crew questioningly; but when he receives only shrugs in reply, he gives an irritated huff and calls, "Action!"

With a nervous smile, I face the three men who made it through all the challenges to stand here before me, hoping to win my heart. *Or at least "win" the show,* I think cynically. After getting to know each of them, I'm well aware of their motivations. Roman is trying to promote his plastic surgery business; Zeke would love to expand his personal training program; and Vincent, well, Vincent still lives at home with his mother and is just looking for the next female who will take care of him.

With those final thoughts in mind, I take a deep breath before addressing them.

"Thank you all for coming tonight. I want you to know how much I appreciate that you each have given your time and attention to this process while I try to find the King who will win my heart."

I pause a moment as motion behind the camera crew catches my eye. I smile as I see a commotion going on nearby, and my heart begins to race. I look back down at the suitors gathered before me, these three men with all their false confidence and arrogance. Not one of them has a fraction of what makes Abe so special.

Once I've given Ryan his dramatic pause, I continue. "All of you came here with a dream in your hearts. I have narrowed down the bachelors, looking for the one of you who actually dreamed of me and who came here with the intentions of finding love. Only one of the men here has succeeded. The rest failed because they came here not to find love, but to find their own fame or pursue their own interests. To most of you, I was only a trophy, your reward for winning a contest."

I fix each of the men with a cold stare, then address each of them individually. "My heart was never a reward for you to win. My love is a responsibility for you to earn, to cherish and to hold dear every day of your life, not put aside on your mantle and be forgotten when you move on to your next endeavor. This is why there is only one of you who I can truly call my King."

I glance over to the cameras again and see that Ryan has moved behind the lighting, out to the source of the earlier disturbance. The cameras are still recording, however, and so I take a deep breath to continue just before Abe comes stomping through the garden scene in his jeans, t-shirt and leather cut.

"Mercy!" he yells, drawing the attention of the three men gathered before me.

"What in the world?"

"Who the hell?"

"What's going on here?"

Everyone begins speaking at once before Abe turns his fearsome glare down on them.

"You know me, you dipshits! Now shut the hell up. I don't want to hear another word from any of you. I only want to hear her," Abe says, pointing a thick finger that trembles slightly up to me at the podium. I nearly laugh out loud when I glance over and see the expression on my mother's face. She's holding her hand to her chest, most likely from Abe's dramatic entrance or his dirty mouth. Probably both.

"Abe, I..." I start to tell him that I heard and saw him coming, and what I was planning to do.

"Mercy, wait," he interrupts me. "Don't say anything yet. Please, I'm begging you...pick me. I know I've been a coward and I don't deserve you. That's why I've never been able to find the guts to tell you that I want you to be mine, not just now, but forever. I love you, Red, and I've never felt this way about anyone in my life. I know I'm not a part of this," he says, waving a hand around the scenery. "But *you* are a part of me. You're the best part of me, a part I didn't know I was missing. And now that I found you, I never want to let go. Please..." he continues as he strides forward, then falls down on both of his knees before me. "I love you, Mercy Daniels. Please choose me."

Clutching the red pin in my fist, I take a step forward and fasten it to the "Beard Rides 10 Cents" shirt that Abe's wearing, rather than put a hole in his beloved leather. "It was always you, Abram Cross. There was never any competition here, and no one else ever had a chance. I love you, Abe, and I only want to be your queen."

Abe gets to his feet and sweeps me off the ground, cradling me to his chest in his thick, muscular arms. I grab his beard gently and guide his lips to mine for a kiss. We stand there together, only interrupted when Ryan suddenly yells, "Cut! That was awesome, everyone! What a finale! No one will be able to see this ending coming. That's a wrap, ladies and gentlemen!"

Abe and I break our kiss long enough to see the three suitors sulking away, looking shell-shocked and demanding explanations from the crew as to what the hell just happened to their finale. As Abe sets me back down on my feet but still embraces me, Ryan and my mother both rush over.

"Abe, right? Nice to meet you," Ryan says in a rush. "Mercy, that was brilliant. Why didn't you tell me what you were planning? I'm going to make some calls tonight and pitch this immediately. They just told me we have some rough scenes of the big guy trying his hands at a few of the competitions too."

"Is this some kind of joke?" my mother demands. "Mercy, you're not seriously..."

"Joseph, Mother. *Joseph*," I repeat while glaring at her not to run her mouth. "Meet Abe. Abe, this is my mother, Loretta Daniels."

"It's, um, a pleasure to meet you, Mrs. Daniels," Abe says when he reaches out and takes her hand to shake it.

My mother eyes him up and down, jaw gaping for several long moments. I brace myself for impact when she finally decides to speak again.

"Well, you're a big one, aren't you?" she says.

"Yes, ma'am. The better to keep your daughter safe."

"And...do you go to church?" she asks.

"I would go with Mercy," Abe answers.

"You don't have to go to church with me," I tell him.

"Don't you know I'd do anything for you?" he reminds me with a grin.

"This is just perfect!" Ryan interrupts. "I'm telling you, with just a little bit of rework on that contract extension, *My Big, Bad, Biker Boyfriend* could be the biggest smash of the fall!"

"What do you think, Abe?" I ask teasingly, guiding his head down for another kiss. "Now that you're my King, are you up for being my big, bad biker boyfriend too?"

"I'm up for anything as long as it involves you, Red. I finally understand what I've been feeling, and this love is something I will never let go."

"Then let's get out of here. There will be plenty of time for you to get interrogated by my mother, and we can deal with the contracts later. Tonight, your queen just wants to take a ride with you."

EPILOGUE

Abe
Several months later...

"What did you decide to do, wear your ugly Christmas tie?" I ask my brother Gabriel when he meets me outside of the church in a suit with snowmen on his bright red tie.

Dark eyes just like mine look me up and down, taking in my black button-down shirt with black jeans and boots, and then he snorts derisively. "You're supposed to wear a suit to church, man, especially on Christmas. I know Mercy has explained this to you at some point."

"I don't own a suit. Hell, she bought me this shirt. The first time I met her and her mom here for the service I wore one of *my* t-shirts. Apparently, some of these old birds were scandalized," I say with a grin as I clap my brother on his arm, then join the line of people slowly making their way into the chapel.

"Mercy and her mom already inside?" Gabe asks.

"Yeah, they're in there with the camera crew, getting some shots of the holiday service for the show," I tell him. "Thanks for agreeing to come with me and be a part of this. I still get a little nervous about the cameras, you know?"

"You afraid you're gonna forget they're watching and try to adjust your junk on film?" Gabe says with a laugh. "I still can't believe Torin agreed to this. He really must be in a better mood lately."

"Yeah, he was cool as long as there were no cameras in any of the club's private areas and no club business got discussed around the crews," I agree. "He knew it was a personal favor to me too. I want Mercy to be successful; and if that means going along with this for a few months, I can deal with it."

"Put your game face on," Gabe says in mock seriousness as he holds the door to the chapel open for me. "Your adoring fans are waiting."

Mercy and her mother are just inside with the camera crew, who instantly focus on my brother and I as we enter. With a huge grin, I stomp over and gather Mercy into a hug, giving her a brief kiss.

"She okay, Red?" I whisper to Mercy.

"My mother will be fine. She's gotten used to you, so meeting Gabe should be easy," Mercy mumbles in reply before breaking our embrace. "Gabe, thank you so much for coming tonight!" Mercy gushes as she gives my brother a hug.

"I wouldn't miss it," Gabe tells her. "I love seeing my brother with you and feeling like a part of your family."

"Well, isn't he a polite one," Mercy's mom says from behind her.

"Gabriel, this is my mother Loretta," Mercy introduces them, using his fancy biblical name before stepping aside to snuggle up to me.

"It's a pleasure to meet you," Gabe says sincerely, holding out his hand to Loretta. "Your daughter is a treasure, and I can see where she gets her looks!"

"Oh, thank you, Gabriel. What a beautiful name for a beautiful face," Loretta says with a smile as she pulls Gabe in for a hug. "I have to tell you it's good to see more of *your kind* joining us here at worship."

Mercy pokes me in the side, and I realize I'm scowling at the mention of *your kind*, but Gabe doesn't seem the least bit flustered. Mercy steps away and takes her mother's arm, turning her towards the rows of pews.

"Shall we go find a place to sit?" Mercy asks, guiding her away under the camera's watchful eye.

Gabe watches them walk away before turning to me and giving me a half-hearted shrug.

"*Your kind*," I snort as I watch Mercy and her mother walk away.

"Abe, it's fine..." my brother tells me quietly.

"I know," I snort. "I just don't like her lumping you in automatically as a biker because you're with me. Hell, you look good in that suit; and if I didn't know you, I'd think you were a lawyer or something."

Gabe just stares at me silently for a long moment before shaking his head and laughing. "Come on, bro, let's get down there with the ladies before they pick up any more super fans like that dude, Joseph. What happened to him anyway? He still in jail?"

"Oh, yeah. Once he got extradited back to North Carolina, he took a plea to three years, which Mercy was happy about. She didn't want to have to go to court and see that little bastard anymore. He won't be a problem for her again. I'm pretty sure I knocked all the love and affection right out of that..."

"Language, please!" Loretta interrupts as we stop beside the pew where she and Mercy are sitting.

"Sorry, Mrs. Daniels," I grumble as I scoot past her to sit with Mercy.

"Sit here, dear," Loretta tells Gabe, patting the bench just beside her. As my brother sits down and adjusts his suit jacket with a smile, I put my arm around Mercy and lean in close to take a deep breath of her mango scent.

"They seem to be getting along well," I whisper.

"I know. Isn't that awesome?" Mercy gushes. "It may just be because we're in church. Mom is always on her best behavior here," she tells me in a low, soft voice.

I watch the camera crews get settled around the area as the producer and his staff walk around, talking to the parishioners and making sure they're ok with being a part of the filming.

"I'll be glad when this part of the show is all over," I grumble, shifting uncomfortably on the hard pew.

"Oh, Abe, tell me the truth. Has my *Big, Bad, Biker Boyfriend* been awful for you? I know you're not used to all of this, and you've been so good about everything," Mercy says, looking worried.

"No, Red, that's not what I meant," I reply. "I'm just ready to get onto the next part of the series."

"The next part?" Mercy asks with an adorable little puzzled crease in her brow.

I catch the gaze of the producer, Ryan, and wave him over to us. "You got that paperwork ready for her to take a look at yet?" I ask him when he slides into the pew beside us.

"Almost!" Ryan says with excitement. "The network suits loved the idea. Mercy, what did you think? Does it sound like something you want to do?"

"What do I think of what?" Mercy says in exasperation, looking between the two of us.

"You didn't ask her yet?" Ryan asks, his eyes widening.

"Well, I wanted to check out the set a little more, see what my brother thought, you know..." I say innocently, waving my arm to encompass the entire church.

"What are you talking about?" Mercy laughs, poking me in the ribs.

"I'm talking about where we should film our *Big, Bad Biker Wedding*...if, you know, that's something you might be interested in doing down the line," I tell Mercy with a grin.

"Are you trying to propose to me right now?" Mercy gasps, her eyes threatening to water.

"Well, I would want you to read the paperwork first, and..." I begin, before Mercy throws her arms around my neck, choking off my words.

"Yes, yes, yes!" Mercy exclaims. "A thousand times, yes," she continues, before grabbing my beard and pulling me in for a kiss.

"Well, that's great!" Ryan says, edging away from us. "I'll make sure we get the paperwork and...yeah, I'll leave you guys alone," he finishes lamely, standing up and nodding to the cameramen to make sure they're capturing everything.

"Oh, god," Mercy says as she breaks our kiss. "I just realized, I'm never going to hear the end of this from Sasha!"

I bark out a laugh before agreeing. "You and me both, Red. Honestly, though, I don't think I would ever let her forget. I want her to remember that she introduced me to you and gave me the gift that the MC always promised — love and a family to call my own. I love you, Red, in ways I never knew I could. Thank you, for everything."

"Stop it, big guy," Mercy tells me as she swipes at her eyes. "You're gonna make me cry in front of the cameras."

"Let it all out, baby," I reassure her. "Your fans will eat it up, and everyone watching will know once and for all that you're my Queen."

The End

ALSO BY LANE HART

Torin's story is now available!

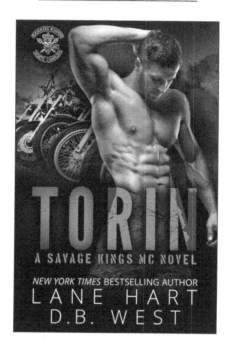

ABOUT THE AUTHORS

New York Times bestselling author Lane Hart and husband D.B. West were both born and raised in North Carolina. They still live in the south with their two daughters and enjoy spending the summers on the beach and watching football in the fall.

Connect with D.B.:
    Twitter: https://twitter.com/AuthorDBWest
    Facebook: https://www.facebook.com/authordbwest/
    Website: https://www.dbwestbooks.com
    Email: dbwestauthor@outlook.com

Connect with Lane:
    Twitter: https://twitter.com/WritingfromHart
    Facebook: http://www.facebook.com/lanehartbooks
    Instagram: https://www.instagram.com/authorlanehart/
    Website: http://www.lanehartbooks.com
    Email: lane.hart@hotmail.com

Join Lane's Facebook group to read books before they're released, help choose covers, character names, and titles of books! https://www.facebook.com/groups/bookboyfriendswanted/

Find all of Lane's books on her Amazon author page!
    Sign up for Lane's newsletter to get updates on new releases and freebies!

Made in the USA
Las Vegas, NV
22 September 2021

30790163R10134